GAS MONEY

Monty McGinnis

GAS MONEY

Monty McGinnis

Tranquility Press, 2022

Tranquility Press
723 W University Ave #300-234
Georgetown TX 78626
tranquilitypress.com

This story is a work of fiction based on real events. Certain long-standing institutions and public offices are mentioned, as well as some real persons; however, they are used in a fictitious manner. The views and opinions expressed herein are those of the characters only and do not necessarily reflect the views and opinions held by individuals on which those characters are based.

ISBN: 978-1-950481-36-1
Library of Congress Control Number: 2022935142

Cataloging in Publication Information
Names: McGinnis, Monty, author.
Title: Gas money / Monty McGinnis.
Description: Georgetown, TX: Tranquility Press, 2022.
Identifiers: LCCN: 2022935142
ISBNs: 978-1-950481-36-1 (trade) | 978-1-950481-37-8 (ebook)
Subjects: LCSH: Oil industry workers—Fiction | Fortune hunters—
Oklahoma—Fiction | Oil fields—Oklahoma—Fiction | Money making
projects—Fiction. GSAFD: Historical fiction | Adventure fiction. LCGFT:
Historical fiction | Social problem fiction | Domestic fiction. BISAC:
FIC084030/FICTION/World Literature/American/20th Century |
FIC045000/FICTION/Family Life/General | FIC002000/FICTION/Action
& Adventure | FIC066000/FICTION/Small Town & Rural
Classifications: LCC PS3613.M3456G376 2022 | DDC 813/.6—dc23
LC record available at https://lccn.loc.gov/2022935142

Dedicated to Sue,

my life editor for the last 58 years

Author's Note

Hustory books leave out much from the amazing stories of fortunes made and lost in the Oklahoma oil industry around the turn of the twentieth century, when the demand for gasoline to fuel the growing number of cars, trucks, and airplanes drove oil production pioneers to produce and refine crude oil. It was the beginning of oil companies still operating today. Few remember the early pioneers—Frank Phillips, W.G. Skelly, Harry Sinclair, and J. Paul Getty. With his four brothers, Frank Phillips began the Phillips Petroleum Company, which made Phillips 66 gasoline.

The boom times turned to bust for many of the early millionaires. Crude oil from these first oil fields was delivered across the Arkansas river from Tulsa, Oklahoma to a refinery built by Tom Cosden. In 1916 it was the largest independent refinery in the world. Tom blew through a net worth of over $50 million by 1925, then moved to east Texas and made a second fortune, only to lose it all in the Depression. Harry Sinclair built the Sinclair Oil Company but lost money in the Teapot Dome scandal and the Depression. He died in 1956 at the young age of 50. Tom Slick discovered the Cushing oil field near Drumright, Oklahoma and made millions, but worked himself to death at 49 years old.

Now, in the twenty-first century, the world faces an energy crisis; yet there is enough natural gas, a cleaner-burning source of energy, in the U.S. to supply our energy needs for decades to come. New production technology using horizontal drilling and fracking techniques have increased supply and satisfied current domestic demand. However, the price is rising due to increased world demand. Overstocks are liquified and the resulting LNG (liquified natural gas) is exported to Europe and other markets. New LNG plants are coming online, and will continue to be commercially viable as the wellhead price rises above $4/MMBTU. A higher price will become the incentive for exploration to access the billions of cubic feet of natural gasin Oklahoma and other places.

This story is about the McCalls, a third-generation Oklahoma family who felt the lure of riches from the discovery of black gold and took big risks to tap into natural gas over forty years ago. Their story takes place midcentury, when energy shortages were widespread. Domestic oil and gas companies struggled to satisfy even half of the U.S. demand. Another boom loomed, not in the search for oil but for the new, clean energy, natural gas. Independent Oklahoma wildcatters will explore three miles deep into the central Oklahoma prairies looking for a huge untapped source of energy and the riches it promises. Will the McCalls become millionaires like their forefathers—or go broke spending millions to reach it?

PART I

Oklahomans in the Oil Patch

Chapter 1

Summer 1969

The yellow station wagon headed toward him boiling up dust from the county gravel road. He was leaning on the picket fence in front of Mrs. Johnston's boarding house anticipating another challenging summer day in the oil patch. Instead of traditional oil field bib-overalls, he wore his Levi's, a grease-stained khaki shirt, and company-required steel-toed work boots. His aluminum hard hat was cradled upside down in his arm with two pairs of work gloves inside.

Will McCall reflected on his summer experience as a roughneck, doing the tough, dirty job of drilling an oil well, known as making hole. It had been hard work, but his persistence over the last several weeks earned him a level of acceptance from the older crew members.

In another week he'd be back at OU to finish his senior year. The summer's labor taught him to appreciate the value of education. With a degree as a mechanical engineer, he would be using his mind to make a living, not his back.

The yellow crew car slid to a stop in front of Will. He climbed into the back seat next to Vernon, the crew member he worked closest with, who taught him the skills of a roughneck. The aroma of oily dirt unique to oil rig drilling crews reminded Will he was still in the oil well drilling business. What would this hot summer day bring?

"Mornin', Vernon. Mornin', Steve."

Steve rode shotgun in the front seat next to their boss, Harold Crowley. Though only a few years older than Will, Steve was already a seasoned roughneck. Will, Vernon, and Steve, along with a mechanic, worked for Harold, the driller.

"Mornin', Mr. Crowley."

"Good mornin', Will," Harold replied, as he turned his station wagon around, heading back to the east-west state highway and main street of Wilburton, Oklahoma.

Vernon, a career roughneck who wore the preferred bib overalls, looked older than his forty years. He had a short, wiry build with dark hair and eyes and a stubbled beard. Will's teammate on the rig floor, he'd often referred to Will as "worm," the oil patch equivalent of a greenhorn, for the first two weeks. Vernon also taught him how to do the dangerous job of a roughneck safely.

A new country and western song, popular with Oklahomans, played on the car radio. Will was about to comment on it when Vernon spoke up.

"That Merle Haggard writes some damn good country songs. 'Okie from Muskogee,' is already a country hit and is putting Muskogee on the map."

"Yep," Will said. "I like it, particularly the reference to the Roughers, the high school football team. We played against them a few years ago and they gave us a good whooping."

"I hear you're goin' back to school soon. Why not stay longer? We're just startin' to have some fun, now that you've made a hand. You've come a long way since joining our crew. Done the job in the grease and mud without complaint. Well, maybe some." He chuckled. "Put up with our 'worm' bullshit and turned your fat into muscle." He gave Will a fist bump to his shoulder.

Will smiled. "Thanks." He took the bump as a gesture of acceptance. Back in high school, he'd been a tough football athlete, playing halfback and defensive back despite his medium height and build. In the three years since, plus this summer in the oil field, he'd added twenty pounds of mostly muscle and grown two inches taller. His blond hair, cut in the popular flattop style, complemented his easy personality.

"That means a lot to me, Vernon, but no, I'm headed back in another week. You've put up with me long enough. I've learned a lot from you guys, but I'm looking forward to finishing my senior year at OU. After working with you all on the rig, I know I want to continue working in the oil and gas business, maybe with a company like Phillips Petroleum. This summer experience will be a plus on my résumé when I interview for a job."

His father had encouraged him to bring his mechanical engineering skills into the family business, but Will didn't see any need for engineering in a business of cleaning and refurbishing salvaged oil production tanks and equipment.

Harold had driven about ten minutes northwest on State Highway 2 when he turned south through a gate onto a private gravel road leading to the oil well drilling site. A small black and white sign on the gate post read *Loffland Brothers Brushy Creek #1*. Diesel engines chugged in the distance. In another quarter mile, the yellow station wagon reached the top of a rise and Will glimpsed the drilling rig's one-hundred-foot-tall derrick. The rig's diesel engines revved louder.

The roar meant the large cable-wound pulley, called a traveling block, was lifting thousands of feet of drill pipe out of the well hole. Several three-joint stands were stacked vertically on the rig floor, leaning against the derrick structure. The morning crew must be making a trip, pulling up all the pipe to put on a new drill bit.

The car had moved on down into a low point in the road out of sight of the rig when Will heard a low thundering sound that vibrated the ground and their station wagon.

"Did you all feel that?" he asked.

After Vernon and Steve responded "Yeah" simultaneously, there was a piercing whoosh, like the sound of an enormous volume of water spraying from an open pipe or hose. The car moved to the top of the next hill, revealing a shocking sight. Drilling mud spewed out the open-ended drill pipe at the rig floor, up and through the top of the derrick, carrying with it dirt and rocks, and showered down over the rig and the surrounding site.

"Holy crap, look," Will shouted out his open window.

"Looks like they've just had a massive gas kick," Steve said, watching out the windshield.

Harold stopped the car. "Damn it to hell. That's a blowout, not a little gas kick. Let's wait and see if they can get it under control. I don't want that shit landing on us and my car."

Vernon added, "They need to get the blowout preventers engaged to shut off the heaviest flow, and then put the Kelly bushing and swivel back on the open drill pipe." He referred to the apparatus that turned with the drill pipe and delivered the man-made mud down the center of the pipe to the bit. "If they can stick it back on the open pipe, it would stop the blowout."

"That's going to be a tough job when it's blowing mud in their face," Will said. "Maybe they should wait until it blows itself down."

"No, too dangerous," Harold said. "After all the mud is blown out, natural gas will follow, and a spark could ignite the gas. Then we've got fire, a much bigger problem."

The morning crew on the rig floor scrambled to stop the spewing mud and get the runaway well under control. The driller picked up the Kelly bushing and swivel from a side station. The rig floormen pushed it over to the open end of the drill pipe at the rig floor where the mud was gushing out like high-pressure water from a big fire hose. Will watched the crew attempt to attach it to the top of the drill pipe to shut off the massive mud flow reaching the top of the derrick. The effort reminded him of trying to attach a spray nozzle to the end of a garden hose with the water running full open.

For a few tense minutes, the rig crew worked to cap the open pipe while the mud sprayed sideways with devastating force. At last, the shower of mud and rocks stopped, leaving a mist of mud drifting to the ground. The rig appeared intact. The crew stood on the rig floor covered in man-made mud.

Harold put the car in gear and moved ahead as the crew sat back in quiet awe of what they just witnessed. He drove over the mud-covered road to the rig, parking next to a travel trailer off to the side. The *Loffland*

Brothers Company name painted on the trailer and car door was now barely legible through the dripping mud. Frank Smith, Loffland Brother's tool pusher, or site boss, used the trailer as an office. He was in charge of the drilling operation 24 hours a day, 7 days a week.

Vernon said, "Well, college boy, I bet we're gonna get to help clean up their mess."

"Glad I brought an extra pair of gloves," Will replied. He got out of the car and waited with his crew for orders, wondering what to expect when the trailer door opened.

Frank Smith stepped out, shouting instructions.

"Harold, keep your crew down here until I can see if everyone is all right and assess the damages." He hurried to the 20-foot-tall stairway leading to the rig floor and climbed mud-covered steps.

Will surveyed the scene. Thick brown drilling mud covered the rig, the extra pipe laying on ground racks, Frank's office trailer, and the surrounding area. Mr. Crowley's station wagon looked like a lone yellow sunflower standing in a muddy field.

A huge mess to clean up, and then what? Try to resume drilling, or pump in cement to seal off the gas pocket? This was going to be a challenging day.

Chapter 2

That same afternoon, Lew McCall called his wife from a gas station in Purcell, Oklahoma, to tell her he'd be home within the hour.

"What's going on with you?" he asked.

"Me? Just washing clothes, running a business, and keeping bill collectors away from the door."

"So a routine day at the McCall house," he said with a hint of sarcasm.

"Yes," Johanna answered. "Where are you?"

"I negotiated a deal for some tanks today. I'm now in Purcell getting gas. Should be home within the hour; and since it's Saturday, and I know you don't want to cook, why don't I go by Smitty's and bring home some barbeque for dinner?"

"Excellent idea, but we only need enough for two. Erin has a date with Phil, so it'll just be you and me."

Lew picked up a pound of beef brisket plus a pint of coleslaw and turned out on the new interstate highway headed north for home in South Oklahoma City, his mind still on the purchase of the day.

We may have to rent a larger trailer to handle these tanks. Or maybe we can get by using a long trailer and winch. Hmm, it might be better to bring two flatbed trailers to pick up the salvage tanks...

When he turned into the gate of their property, he passed a red Camaro coming out. He didn't recognize the car but Erin's boyfriend, Phil, was driving and Erin was waving from the passenger seat. He touched the brake pedal, prepared to stop, but the car sped on out to the street.

Lew continued past the shop at the front of the two-acre property near the street entrance to a grassy half-acre parcel beyond it, where the family doublewide trailer sat.

Johanna greeted him at the door with a welcome kiss and hug, then leaned back with a smile. "Glad you're home."

Lew kept her in his arms. His wife had her German father's stout frame but inherited her French mother's fair skin and dark hair. "I saw Erin and Phil leaving in a red Camaro. Where are they going?"

"Nice car, huh? Apparently, he traded in his old Ford. I think this one is two or three years old but it looks almost new. They're going for a burger and then to a show."

He sniffed the air and raised his eyebrows to her.

"Please, no lecture on my smoking." She pulled from his arms and took the sack of brisket and slaw. "Thanks for bringing dinner, honey."

Lew shut the door behind him. "Okay," he said, wagging his finger. "I quit once, and you've quit twice. Why don't you try again? Third time's a charm, you know. Maybe it would help to buy some of that gum that's supposed to help you kick the nicotine habit."

"I've been cutting back, and yes." She held her hand up as if taking an oath. "I'll try the gum. Now go sit down. I'll get you a beer and fix a couple of plates." She handed him a Coors from the fridge. "When you called, you said you made a deal for some tanks. Are they in good condition? Do you think we can turn them quickly?"

"Yeah, they're in good shape. It won't take much to clean 'em up, but finding a buyer during this slow economy may take a while. Paul and I will bring them back to the shop this week." He dropped into his recliner and began removing his boots while Johanna divided the sliced barbeque onto two paper plates.

"Paul called me from the shop a couple of hours ago," she said. "Something about a paint problem on the big separator unit for Kerr-McGee. Do you want to check on it while there's still daylight?"

"Maybe after we eat. I'm pooped and hungry." He took a swig of beer as she set a tray holding a paper plate of brisket and coleslaw in his lap.

Johanna changed the subject. "I'm getting excited about the new house now that it's taking shape. The builder called today to report that they've finished the interior framing. Can we go out there tomorrow or next week? I know we're busy, but we need to look it over while it's easy to make changes. With Will about graduate and Erin off to college this month, soon it'll be just you and me." She walked by him with her tray and leaned over to give him a peck on the top of his bald head.

"I agree," Lew said. "After living in this mobile home for years, it'll be great to be in a nice brick house. And weekend farming might be fun since we won't have to dependent on it for food and clothing. You know, owning land is my idea of success. It's a solid family asset that'll increase in value for our kids and grandkids."

Johanna took a swig of beer before replying. "Yes, it's an excellent investment, but I'm looking forward to the wide-open spaces of eighty acres with a fenced backyard and a patio for cookouts. When we sold half of your father's acreage, there was talk about the land your grandfather, Thomas, originally owned and what your father inherited. What was that all about?"

"Heck, I don't remember. That was years ago. I expect it was about ownership of the other quarter section owned decades ago by Grandfather Thomas. It's turned over several times since then." Lew sat back with a thoughtful stare. "I remember when I left the farm. Dad told me if anything happened to him, I should look into the sale and deed transfer on that acreage. The papers are in the safe deposit box with the other financial records on both properties. We need to dig them out and see if there's something we've overlooked."

The long summer daylight was fading when they finished their indoor picnic. Lew started to nod off as Johanna picked up the used napkins and paper plates.

"Hey, why don't you go to bed. You can check out the paint issue tomorrow."

Lew grunted a sound of agreement. Pulling himself from the recliner, he headed to the bedroom, boots in hand.

The next morning Lew read the Sunday paper over coffee on the cedar deck he'd built in front of their mobile home. A popular new song played on a transistor radio next to him. It was the product of the sixties' free love and psychedelic crowd, but he liked it.

The screen door opened and his youngest daughter, Erin, still in her pajamas and slippers, stepped out and slumped into a folding chair across from her father.

"Well, good morning, Erin. I didn't expect to see you up so early this morning. Did you and Phil have a good time last night? I like that red car he's driving."

"Nice, huh? He traded his old Ford for the Camaro, with help from his father. He says he'll pay his father back with money he's going to earn working part-time at his dad's bank. We went to the movie but spent most of the time talking about the future. Hey, isn't this a song from the musical Hair?"

"It is. 'The Age of Aquarius.' It may surprise you, but I like it. The 5th Dimension harmonize beautifully."

"Me, too. Careful, Dad, someone might think you're hip."

"I came out to talk about school. Here I am about to start college but don't even know what I want to do the rest of my life. I'm having second thoughts about going to college at all. I know you and Mom have saved for my education, but you know I've never been an A student. It might be a waste of money."

Lew lowered the sports section and reached to turn down the radio. "Erin, money spent on education is never waisted. A lot of successful people made Bs and Cs in school. President Eisenhower graduated in the bottom half of his class at West Point, but his talent was organization and problem solving. Maybe you just need to find your talent and a career to get excited about."

"I'm envious of Will," she said. "He's always made good grades and is about to get his engineering degree. I just don't see me doing that."

Lew folded the paper in his lap, anticipating the

start of a more serious father-daughter discussion, but Johanna appeared at the screen door.

"Did I hear you mention Will?" she asked. "I'm going to call him later today to find out when he plans to come home. He needs to spend a little time here at home before he goes back to school, and we haven't heard from him in a week or more. Maybe he's found a girlfriend in the Ouachita mountains." Smiling, she went back inside.

Erin rolled her eyes. "Oh, good grief, I hope not. Seriously? I do know he's not planning to join the family business. Isn't that disappointing?"

"A little, sure," Lew answered. "But there's still time. He might change his mind someday. We want him to follow his dream, whatever it is. That goes for you, too. We'll always help you to follow your dream, find the right path for you. But the best chance for success, in whatever you decide to do, is to complete your education."

"I know that's what you think is best, but me and Phil have been talking about getting married. We've worked out a plan."

Lew sat up straight and gritted his teeth, trying to think what to say.

Erin kept her head down, avoiding eye contact as she continued. "He's been working part-time in his father's bank, and he'll continue until he finishes his degree in finance and accounting. I can get a waitressing job, so we have money to live on."

Stunned at his youngest daughter talking about marriage, Lew hesitated, searching for the right words to reply. Johanna interrupted a father-daughter discussion he wasn't prepared for when she opened the screen door again. "Would you two come in here and help me get breakfast on the table?"

Lew used the momentary pause to excuse himself. "I need to go over to the shop and check something." Then, quietly, he said to Erin, "A marriage discussion needs more time and your mother's input. We'll talk about it later when we can include her."

Erin showed her dad a frown and rose to go in.

Johanna raised her voice from the kitchen. "Lew, there's nothing over in that shop that can't wait until after breakfast."

"I need to inspect the paint problem you mentioned yesterday, on the Kerr-McGee unit. It's one of the biggest rebuild projects we've done and they're a big customer. It's got to be right. I'll be back before you can get breakfast on the table."

He was already off the deck, hurrying to the large metal McCall's Production Equipment fabrication shop. What if the Kerr-McGee project wasn't ready to ship tomorrow, as promised? The job was a large assembly of two production vessels with connecting piping big enough to require a flatbed semi to haul it.

He pushed open the large double doors of the fabrication shop and flipped the master switch to overhead lights. The huge double-barreled gas separator sat in the center, next to the shop office. He was momentarily relieved. It looked finished, with a shiny coat of light gray paint. Lew walked around the separator, surveying the large unit.

It looks good. The paint was smooth throughout except for two white chalk circles near the top. The assembly of stacked vessels and piping, mounted on a large steel frame, was too tall for him to identify the paint issue indicated by the chalk circles..

He found a step ladder nearby and dragged it over to the large assembly. Opening the ladder sideways to the large steel beam base, he climbed to the last step near the top. Now he could see the gray paint inside the chalk circles had bubbled. He leaned forward for a closer look. Steading himself with his left hand on the curved vessel surface, he reached with his right hand to touch the paint inside one of the circles.

The paint felt soft, not adhering to the steel underneath. "Damn," he blurted out. He extended his reach, focusing on the paint, trying to scrape the bubbled area with his thumb. The ladder slowly tipped under his feet. When his left hand began to slide on the smooth curved vessel, the ladder moved aside with his feet. Suddenly, there was nothing to hold on to.

He was going down, and it was going to hurt.

Erin sat at the table staring at nothing, wondering how to broach the subject of marrying Phil to Mom. She didn't look forward to the conversation.

Johanna stepped to the back door and hollered toward the shop. "Lew, breakfast is ready."

No answer came back.

"Erin, would you call over to the shop and tell your father breakfast is ready?"

She went to the shop intercom phone next to the kitchen counter and dialed 1-2 on the rotary pad. After a few moments she hung up and said, "He's not picking up."

"Go over to the shop and see what's keeping him."

Grumbling under her breath, Erin slipped into a pair of leather sandals, stepped out the screen door and down off the deck, and walked to the open shop doors. "Dad, breakfast is ready."

No answer. She entered the shop. "Dad. Where are you?"

It was too quiet. No response.

She walked around the large assembly of vessels and piping to the back side. Still no sign of him. She circled around toward the shop office and noticed the legs of a step ladder on its side on the ground. Then she saw her father draped over the top of the ladder.

"Dad? Dad!"

He lay completely still. She shook his shoulder. "Dad, are you all right?" Still no response. Then she noticed under his head what looked like a small pool of blood. Her hand went to her mouth as she took in a deep breath, then she turned and ran out the open double doors shouting, "Mom! Mom! Come quick. Dad's hurt!"

Johanna came to the screen door. "What happened?"

Erin's words tumbled out. "I don't know. He's lying on the shop floor, not moving, and he doesn't answer me. I think he fell off a ladder."

"Come inside and call Dr. Blake. His number is on the wall by the phone. I'll go look after your father and pick up the phone extension in the shop." She spoke calmly, but Erin saw the fear in her eyes before she turned away and hurried to the shop.

<><><>

Johanna found Lew laying on the folded-up step ladder near the base of the large Kerr-McGee unit. His head was bleeding and there was blood on the edge of the beam base of the large assembly. She pressed her fingers to his neck and found a pulse—so weak it pushed her to the edge of panic. Carefully, she rolled him off the ladder and stepped a few feet to a table with a stack of clean rags. Folding several into a pad, she placed them between the gash on his head and the ground, trying to stop the blood flow.

She moved the ladder away and went into the shop office to pick up the extension phone. She heard Erin say, "Can you call an ambulance?"

The woman's voice on the other end said, "Of course; give me your address."

After giving it, Erin said, "Mom? Are you there? This is Dr. Blake's answering service. She paged him to call us as soon as possible and she's calling for an ambulance."

Johanna replied as calmly as she could. "Okay, good. Now go unlock the front gate so they can get in. I'll wait here for Dr. Blake's call."

She hung up and went back to Lew. He was still unconscious. She checked his pulse. It seemed even weaker than a few moments ago.

"Lew. Lew, can you hear me?" No response.

Johanna jumped at the sudden ringing of the phone in the silent shop. She described Lew's condition to Dr. Blake and said he'd probably fallen and hit his head.

"Stay with him, and stay calm," the doctor said. "An ambulance will be there soon to take him to St. Anthony's Hospital. Just follow the ambulance and I'll meet you there."

When she got back to Lew, tears blurred her vision. "Lew McCall, don't you leave me. I can't do all this by myself. I need you."

Erin returned, crying. "Mom? Is he going to be all right?"

Johanna couldn't answer the question. She'd break down if she tried. Instead she said, "The ambulance is coming, and Dr. Blake will meet us at the hospital. Did you open the front gate?"

With tears running down her face, Erin sniffled and nodded.

"Good." Johanna felt her own tears well up and swallowed hard. "Go out to the front gate and lead the ambulance here when they arrive."

Erin stared at her mother for a moment, then ran through the double doors toward the front gate. Soon, Johanna heard an approaching siren.

Chapter 3

In rural Midwest City that same Sunday morning, Stephanie and Charley Arnold awoke to his musical alarm clock. Stephanie rolled across the bed and put her arm around him but he turned away from her and got up.

"What's your hurry?" she said. "It's Sunday and quiet. Crystal's still asleep. We can have a few minutes together."

"Yeah, but Dad was on my case yesterday about not getting more water hauled last week, so I promised to pick up wastewater at the Reynolds lease this morning."

"Tell JD Sunday's a family day. Hauling wastewater isn't an urgent, seven-day job. Who loses money if you pick it up tomorrow?"

"You're right, but he's the boss." Charley shoved his shirttail into his pants.

"You didn't care about his reaction when we left school and got married. Why so intimidated now?"

"Look, he's supported us with this house and gave me a job when I couldn't find anything else." He went across the hall into the bathroom.

Stephanie raised her voice so he'd hear her. "Oh, sure, a two-bedroom frame house on Arnold Oil and Gas land, and we had to borrow money to make it livable."

Crystal, their three-year-old daughter, started crying. Stephanie got up and wrapped a robe about her medium frame and one-time curvaceous figure. She pulled a comb through her shoulder-length blond hair as she walked to the smaller bedroom to pick up her daughter.

"Come on, sweety." Then she shouted in the direction of the bathroom. "Do you want me to fix you some breakfast?"

Charley came to the kitchen as Stephanie placed a bowl of Cheerios in front of Crystal, who sat in a booster seat. "Just make me a thermos of coffee and I'll pick up a breakfast roll on the way." He sat at their farmhouse kitchen table and drummed his fingers while the coffee percolated.

Stephanie sat across from him. "When are we going to work for ourselves? This truck driving for a few bucks an hour doesn't cut it. We're never gonna get ahead this way. As long as we're working for your obnoxious and bullying father, we'll be making peanuts, struggling to buy groceries and pay off loans. Now, if we had another truck, we could do some hauling of our own. Start our own service business."

"Well, that ain't gonna happen today. I gotta get going." He grabbed his pickup truck keys and started out the door.

"Hold up, big boy, you'll want this coffee." Stephanie filled his thermos. "When do you think you'll be home?"

Charley turned sheepishly. "Thanks. I should be back before noon." He climbed into his truck and sped away.

She watched him, continuing to worry about their predicament.

GAS MONEY

What does it take to start our own business and work for ourselves? We can't keep running ourselves ragged day to day, working for JD for just enough to keep our head above water.

Chapter 4

The empty ambulance that had carried Lew still sat in the driveway at St. Anthony's hospital when Johanna and Erin arrived. It was a crowded emergency room after a warm Saturday night, filled with the typical personal accidents, plus a feverish teenager and a crying baby. They hurried to a window with a *Check In* sign.

Johanna called to a young woman in a nurse's uniform. "I'm Johanna McCall. They brought my husband here in the ambulance."

The nurse replied, "Yes, Mrs. McCall, he's in an exam room and trauma doctors are with him."

"Can we see him?" Johanna asked.

Before the nurse replied, Johanna heard Dr. Blake's familiar voice behind her. "I'm here, Johanna." She felt his hand on her back.

The young nurse answered Johanna coldly. "No, I'm sorry. Please wait in this room. I'll let the trauma team know you're here, and the doctor will come out after their initial examination."

Dr. Blake moved around Johanna and Erin to the window. "I'm Dr. Blake, Mr. McCall's physician. What trauma room is he in?"

"Trauma room number two, Dr." She turned back

to Johanna. "Mrs. McCall, I'll need to get Mr. McCall's personal and insurance information."

Dr. Blake turned to go through double doors and called back to Johanna. "I'll check on him and let you know how he's doing."

Frantically, Johanna opened her purse and found the worn leather wallet she'd grabbed from Lew's pocket as the attendants loaded him in the ambulance and pulled out a paper card titled Blue Cross Blue Shield.

The nurse took it and said, "Thank you. Please take a seat and a doctor will be out to talk to you soon."

Holding her hand, Johanna led Erin to empty chairs on a side wall, where they sat stunned and fearful of what might be next. Johanna thought it must be at last noon, but a clock on the wall read only nine fifteen.

Erin asked, "Is Dad going to be okay?"

Johanna silently put an arm around her and pulled her close.

After a long ten minutes, a young man in a white jacket appeared through the double doors next to the main desk, with Dr. Blake following.

Is he the ER trauma doctor? He's closer to Erin's age than Dr. Blake's.

"McCall?" he called out.

Johanna raised her hand, and they both jumped from the chairs and walked over to him. "How is he?" She looked past the youngster to Dr. Blake. His eyes met hers but his expression revealed little.

The ER doctor extended his hand. "Mrs. McCall, I'm Dr. Wilson. Let's go in here." He pushed through the double doors and into a cubicle with a table and chairs. "Please, sit down. I've been examining Mr. McCall and have discussed his condition with Dr. Blake. I'm afraid your husband is critical. The blow to his head fractured his skull. We're trying to determine the damage to his brain, and we'd like your approval to do a spinal tap. It's a procedure to see if there's blood in his spinal column. It can help us determine the extent of the head trauma."

"How is it done?"

"We insert a syringe and draw fluid from his spinal column. If it's clear, any hemorrhage may be local and treatable, with a good chance for recovery. However, if we find blood in the spinal fluid, it will mean a major brain hemorrhage, very difficult to treat. Can you tell me how he hit his head?"

"I think Lew fell off a ladder and hit his head on a steel I-beam." She admitted to being unsure since no one witnessed the fall.

"So, the fall was from a height of about six feet?" he asked.

"Yes, I think so."

"That's consistent with his head injury. We need to do the spinal tap as soon as possible. Do we have your permission?"

"Yes, please go ahead with the test. Is he awake? Can we see him?"

Dr. Blake answered, "He's not conscious, Johanna, and the test will only take a few minutes. Then you can come back. We've given him medication to reduce the pressure and swelling, which may allow him to regain consciousness if the injury isn't too severe." He stood and placed a steady hand on her shoulder. "I'll come back when we've finished the test and know more."

Again, the minutes seemed like hours before Dr. Blake returned. He motioned Johanna and Erin to follow him as he walked into a small, dark conference room.

They entered as he switched on the overhead lights. "Let's sit here for a moment."

Johanna sensed bad news coming and braced herself for the flood of emotion about to hit. She sat down, Erin beside her, gripping her hand tightly. The doctor pulled a chair closer.

"I'm so sorry, Johanna. The news is not good. The spinal fluid contained blood, showing a severe brain hemorrhage. His heart is weak, so we're giving him oxygen to help his breathing. Before we can treat the head trauma, we would need to find the source of the bleeding. His chances for recovery are low. We can take measures to support his heart, but his brain continues to swell from the trauma of the hemorrhage and will cease functioning soon. I'm so sorry. There is little more we can do."

"What about an x-ray to locate the damage?"

"With the amount of hemorrhaging and swelling, it's difficult to pinpoint the location of the damage. We'd have do exploratory brain surgery, which itself is risky and adds to the trauma, putting his life at more risk."

Erin buried her head in her mother's shoulder, sobbing.

Johanna pulled a tissue from the box on the table, fighting back a complete collapse. "Can we see him? We need to see him."

"Of course. Follow me."

A deep pain took root in Johanna's throat and chest. She gripped Erin's hand, and Erin's other hand clung to Johanna's arm as they followed Dr. Blake.

He led them through the double doors to an examination cubicle where another young ER doctor stood beside the table holding Lew, who wore an oxygen mask and wires attached to his chest. The wires connected to a monitor nearby, displaying his pulse, blood pressure, and other vital data. The yellow pulse line on a small black screen showed a regular, shallow heartbeat. Clearly, he was very weak.

Johanna lifted his hand in both of hers. "Lew, if you can hear me, I love you." She squeezed his hand with both of hers, then released one to cover her sobbing nose and mouth with a tissue. She turned to the doctor. "Is he in pain?"

"No," the young doctor replied. "We've given him medication to relieve any pain. Would you like to sit? I'll get you a chair." He moved to pull a chair from near the curtain at the entrance.

Johanna shook her head. She couldn't overcome the pain in her throat to speak. Erin sniffed back tears. The room was otherwise silence except for the constant beeps from the monitor. Suddenly the monitor changed from *beep, beep, beep* to a constant piercing alarm and the graph flattened into a straight line.

The young doctor turned off the monitor. "I'm so sorry, he's gone."

"No, no! Lew? Lew!" Johanna and Erin sobbed uncontrollably. Johanna's knees buckled. Dr. Blake caught her and helped her to sit in the chair, as she continued to cling to Lew's hand. Erin hugged her from behind.

A nurse glanced at a clock on the wall and wrote on a clipboard, then left the room with the young doctor. Dr. Blake stayed beside Johanna and Erin.

In her inconsolable grief, the questions in Johanna's mind were relentless. *Why him? Why us? What do I do now?*

Erin leaned on the chair, crying in her hands.

The young doctor returned. He held out a card. "This has both my number and the hospital number. Stay as long as you like. There's no hurry, but we'll need to know your plans for Mr. McCall. Let me know if you need anything."

Johanna shook her head.

"Why don't you let me drive you both home?" Dr. Blake said.

Again Johanna shook her head. "Thank you, but we'll be okay, and Erin can drive. Thank you for coming." She kissed Lew's hand and placed it gently back on his chest.

Johanna looked up one more time at Lew, then took Erin's hand. They left the treatment room and walked through the waiting area toward the emergency room exit. She glanced at the clock on the wall. It was 10 a.m., but it seemed to her the day was over. Her life was over. Walking quickly to escape the unbearable hospital trauma, the events of the morning were mixed with thoughts of a future without Lew.

She needed to call Stephanie and Will. Stephanie would be at home, but Will was somewhere in Eastern Oklahoma on an oil rig. *Erin can call his boardinghouse when we get home and leave a message for him to call when he gets back from his shift.*

Johanna remembered the phone on the wall in the waiting area. She stopped, holding Erin back, and turned toward the phone. "Erin, I'm going to call your sister. Get the car and pick me up at the front door."

Erin nodded and went on ahead to the car. Johanna picked up the wall phone receiver and dialed Stephanie's number.

When her daughter answered, Johanna blurted out, "Your father fell in the shop this morning and we had to call an ambulance to take him to St. Anthony's Hospital."

"Oh, no. Is he okay? Is it serious?"

"Yes, but I don't want to talk about it on the phone. Erin is with me, and we're leaving the hospital now. Meet us at home. You can bring Crystal if you need to."

"Charley had to haul water at a well site, but he should be home within the hour. I'll come over then. He can stay with Crystal."

When Johanna and Erin arrived back at their doublewide trailer home, the Mr. Coffee machine was still on, coffee ash burned into the glass bottom of the pot. Erin quickly unplugged the device, found an old percolator coffee maker, and set about making more coffee. "I'll make some coffee and finish the breakfast you started earlier. You should try to find the number for Will's boardinghouse and leave a message for him to call home."

Johanna slumped on the end of the couch near the end table with a phone. She had placed a note beside the phone with the number of the Will's boardinghouse the day he left town. The thought of calling him with the bad news caused tears to well up in her eyes. "I don't think I can call without getting too upset."

A few minutes later, Erin put a plate of scrambled eggs and toast on the coffee table in front of her mother and took the note with Mrs. Johnston's boardinghouse phone number. She went to the wall phone and left a brief message with Mrs. Johnston for Will to call home as soon as possible.

Chapter 5

Stephanie paced the floor, her irritation ramping up to anger. It was noon and Charley still wasn't back. *He should be home by now. I've got to go find out what's happening with Dad.*

Within minutes, his truck pulled into the gravel driveway.

She watched him take two steps onto the front porch and toss his hard hat rattling into a plastic chair. He entered without saying a word and plopped down on a well-worn couch set against the front window.

"Damn, it's hot out there. I need a beer!"

"Good afternoon to you, too!" Stephanie snapped. "What took you so long? You said you'd be back by noon."

"I told you I had to haul water at the Reynolds lease this morning." He pulled a pack of cigarettes from his shirt pocket.

She stepped to the refrigerator, pulled out a Coors, and held it out, patiently waiting while he lit a cigarette. "I need you to watch Crystal for a while. Mom called and said Dad had an accident in the shop. She wants me to come over there right away. I'll call you later, okay?"

"Yeah, sure." He took the can from her. "What happened? Is he all right?"

"She had to take him to the hospital, but I don't know any details. I need to get over there and find out what happened. I'll call you when I know more."

Stephanie grabbed her purse and sunglasses and charged out the door. It took less than fifteen minutes to drive from her house in Midwest City to the McCall doublewide trailer home.

Her mother was sitting on the couch when Stephanie walked in and said, "What happened? How's Dad? Is he okay?"

Johanna stood and came to her with open arms, choking back tears. "Dad fell from a ladder and hit his head. We got him to the hospital, but he didn't survive the head injury."

Stephanie tried to absorb the shocking news as her mother hugged her. "What? What are you saying? Dad died?" The shocking news took her breath away, and tears filled her eyes. Johanna squeezed her tighter.

"What happened? Why?" she cried.

Johanna backed away, her eyes filled with tears. "It was a freak accident. We don't really know exactly how it happened. He was alone in the shop, just a freak accident. We think he climbed a ladder to inspect some paint problems on a large separator unit and fell."

Stephanie took a Kleenex from her sister's hand and continued to sob. "So, the ladder didn't break?"

"No," her mother said. "He either slipped or leaned too far to one side and lost his balance. When he fell, he hit the back of his head on a steel beam. We called for the ambulance and got him to the hospital. The doctors said he fractured his skull, which caused a massive stroke. He never regained consciousness. We were with him for a few minutes before he died."

For a moment no one said anything, then Johanna said, "Sit. Would you like something to drink?"

Stephanie was sobbing too hard to answer. Erin walked over and handing her a bottle of Coke, then gave her a gentle hug. Stephanie choked back her sobs enough to drink the Coke.

Johanna lit a Marlboro. "Erin called the boardinghouse where Will is staying and left a message for him to call home. I think he finishes his shift at four."

Chapter 6

After the blowout Harold's crew cleaned up and recaptured the hole. They called Halliburton to cement the gas pocket and ordered a whipstock—a joint of pipe with an angled slot designed to take the bit in a different direction. Today, Will and the men were pulling the drill string to conect the whipstock joint.

"Coming down," Harold warned, then released the brake on the traveling block. The traveling block with its multiple loops of steel cable descended slowly, carrying the elevator, designed to clamp around the shoulder of the last joint at the end of the string so the string could be picked up.

Will recognized the misalignment of the elevator and drill pipe sticking up at the floor. He needed to grab the elevator's handles and push the it back over the pipe before it reached the pipe shoulder, and hold it in position as it fell beside the pipe end.

"Pull the handles together to latch it under the shoulder," Vernon instructed.

Will attempted the move but underestimated the force required. The elevator bounced with a clang off the top of the pipe extending above the floor. Harold hit the brake, leaving the elevator swinging loose.

"Okay, go ahead and latch 'em," Vernon shouted.

"I know." Will said. "The damn elevators aren't exactly in line with the hole. I underestimated how hard to push back and to the left, so it won't hit the pipe shoulder."

Will got the elevator latched, and Harold lifted the drill pipe string. When three 30-foot joints of pipe were above the floor, wedges called slips held the pipe string at the floor. The crew used the large tongs like massive pipe wrenches to break apart the 90-foot-tall stand of three joints and set them aside.

Harold brought the elevator down again. This time, Will was ready. When the handles came into reach, he grabbed them with both hands and gave a hard shove. The open elevator sides cleared the top of the pipe.

Clang! The left handle hit the pipe shoulder.

"Arrgh!" Will let out a painful cry and his reflexes jerked his left hand back. The elevator continued to drop into position below the shoulder. Seeing the open jaws, he reached for one handle with the fingers of his left hand, then pulled hard on the right handle to get the elevator latched. Engines roared as Harold lifted the pipe string again.

Vernon shouted over the roar, "That get your hand?"

Will held his left hand with the right. "No, damn it! My thumb. It got smashed on top of the pipe."

"Pull off your glove. Let's see if it's still attached."

Still cradling his left hand, hoping the pain would lessen, Will slowly slipped the glove off. The thumb was nearly flat and the skin a pale white. A small amount of blood dripped out of a split in the skin at the first knuckle. He squeezed his fingers and thumb painfully slow.

"Damn! That hurt."

"You're lucky it's still connected," Vernon said. "I've seen a smash like that break a finger in two."

When the pipe string reached the top, Harold set the brake and throttled the engines. "Come over here. Let's take a look."

In the doghouse, Will showed he could move the now swelling, bleeding thumb.

"Let's put a tight wrap on that knuckle to stop the bleeding and give your thumb some support," Harold said. "Think you can keep at it? We've got about an hour before relief is here."

"Yeah, I can finish the shift."

"Then we'll put some ice on it for the drive back to town." Harold reached into a drawer in the doghouse and pulled out a bottle of aspirin. "Here, take four. They should help the pain."

Vernon offered, "I'll take over the elevator. You take the back-up tong."

"Thanks. I can swing and push the tong with the heel of my hand easier than pulling the elevator handles."

At four the evening crew arrived, and Harold's crew headed back to town with Will's thumb wrapped in a rag of crushed ice.

When Harold stopped the station wagon in front of Mrs. Johnston's boardinghouse, he said, "You need to get a doctor to look at that thumb. I'll get somebody from the other crew to do a double shift in your place tomorrow. Call me if the doc says it's more serious and you can't continue."

"It should be okay," Will said bravely. "I'll plan on continuing after going to the doctor, but I'll call you for sure, either way."

He went around back and opened the kitchen door to find Mrs. Johnston frying chicken. "Afternoon, Mrs. Johnston. That smells fantastic."

Without looking, she said, "It's for the Smith family at my church. Mr. Smith works in the oil field and recently crushed his hand in a pipe accident. Broke several bones. Now he can't work for several weeks, or maybe never again at that job."

She turned around and her eyes fell to the fat, ice-packed rag wrapped on his left hand and thumb. She reached for his arm. "What in the world happened here?"

"I smashed my thumb. The ice on it helps, but I may need to get a better bandage. I smashed it hard, and it might still bleed a little. My driller thinks I should see a doctor in case it's broken."

"Well?" she said with a stern face. "Let's get that rag off and see what needs to be done."

After removing the iced rag and cleaning his hand and thumb, Mrs. Johnston retrieved some iodine from the cabinet. "This is going to sting, but it's important to keep infection out."

After the painful first aid, Will put more ice on his thumb.

"I almost forgot," Mrs. Johnson said. "Your sister called today and asked you to call her as soon as you get back from work. You can use the hall phone, but please keep it short since it's long distance."

Will dialed O for the operator and gave her the number in Oklahoma City. The phone rang several times before Erin answered.

"Hi Erin, it's me. What's going on?"

"It's Dad," her quivering voice blurted out. "He fell

in the shop this morning, and he's...he's...gone." Will could barely decipher her words over her crying. "He fell and hit his head."

"Gone? What do you mean, gone?" His mind refused to understand.

"He died, Will. He died." She sniffled. "We need you to come home. Can you come home?"

For a moment Will couldn't utter a word as the choking lump in his throat and a growing pain in his chest exceeded the pain in his thumb. Then, with a deep breath, questions came. "Fell and hit his head? I don't understand. What happened?"

Erin sniffed again. He could tell she was struggling to talk through her sobs. "We don't really know. No one was with him, but we think he fell off a ladder and hit his head on a beam that was at the base of the big thing they were painting. Just come on home as soon as you can."

"I'm on my way. I need to pack my stuff, and then it'll take me about three hours to get there. Maybe between nine and ten tonight."

He hung up and walked back into the kitchen. Mrs. Johnston was still frying chicken.

"I've got to go home," he said through a clenched jaw, and turned to go back to his room.

She followed him to his room. "Bad news?"

Sitting on the bed, he held back tears while repeating the brief news of his dad's accidental death. "I've got to go home, and I doubt I'll come back. I need to call Harold and tell him, too."

"Oh, my goodness! Bless your heart." Mrs. Johnston put her arm around his shoulder. "I'm so sorry. I'm going to fix you a plate of chicken. I know you're famished, and you have a long drive ahead of you. Go on and call your driller while I'm dishing it up."

The call to Harold was difficult because Will had to say the words, "My father died." Saying it shocked him all over again. It didn't seem real.

Will knew his leaving would be a problem for Harold and the crew, but he didn't have a choice. Besides, he had less than two weeks remaining on the job.

"That's too bad," Harold said. "Your replacement was due in week anyway, and might be able to get here sooner. What with your dad's death and your thumb, I guess you don't need to worry about coming back."

Harold's comments reminded him of the pain in his thumb, and his verbalizing the two events pushed Will's mind from sadness to anger as he hung up.

Why? Just when things are going so well. He threw his clothes into his duffel bag, stuffing madly while gritting his teeth, holding back the urge to cry out loud. His summer was over, and a cloudy future lay ahead. *What now? School? The family business?*

Within minutes he'd loaded the back seat of his '56 Chevy and was back in Mrs. Johnston's kitchen. She had several pieces of fried chicken on a plate with some home-grown green beans.

"Sit and eat," she directed. "I'll get you a Coca Cola from the icebox." She got the bottle of Coke and then pulled a pill bottle from the cupboard next to the icebox and set it on the table. "Here, take two of these. They're stronger than aspirin and will take the edge off the pain in your thumb. It's going to get worse before you get back home."

Will inhaled the chicken he would have loved to

slowly savor. His mouth enjoyed the many flavors of its fried crust, but his physical pain and the shocking news about his dad diverted his mind from the overall goodness. He thanked Mrs. Johnston for the supper, the pills, and allowing him to stay in her guest room for the summer.

"I enjoyed having you here, Will, and I know you'll do well at whatever you decide to do after school. This is going to be a difficult time, but you'll get past it. You have your whole life ahead of you. My prayers are with you and your family to find peace."

Will waved to her as he got into his red and white Chevy. It was just before six when he pulled onto the gravel road heading to Highway 270 and west to McAlester. His thumb hurt like hell. He hoped Mrs. Johnston's pills would kick in soon. With some luck, he'd make it home by nine.

Chapter 7

Will reached home about nine-thirty that evening. His mother met him at the door.

"I'm so glad you're home." She hugged him the way only mothers do. Almost immediately, she commented on his bandaged hand. "What happened to your hand?" She lifted it gently, examining the ice-packed thumb.

"It's my significant screwup this summer, and it just happened today. I smashed my thumb working on the oil rig. I think it's just swollen. What happened to Dad?"

Stephanie stepped up to give him a hug, offering a tearful repeat of the accident. Not much different from what Erin had said. Will's many questions, most about why, went unanswered. Like his mother and sister, Will shook his head. "Just a freak accident" was a difficult explanation to accept.

"Have you all talked about a funeral service?" he asked.

"We brought it up, but Mom is having a difficult time facing that subject," Stephanie answered.

"I haven't been able to think about arranging a funeral. I don't want to," Johanna said. "I don't know what Lew would want. We never talked about it—thought there'd be time to handle that when we got old."

She walked to the kitchen counter and picked up her pack of cigarettes and lighter. After a long drag and then exhaling a long plume of smoke, she continued, "We never expecting anything like this. It's just not right. How am I going to do this?"

"What about a will?" he asked. "I remember you saying something about that a few years ago."

"Yes, Sam Buchanan wrote our wills three years ago. He also did the legal work when we established the business. I'll call Sam first thing tomorrow morning; he'll know what to do."

Stephanie spoke up. "I need to get back home." She walked over and kissed her mother on the forehead. "I'll talk to you more tomorrow."

"I'll follow you out," Will said. "I need to get my bags."

Walking to their cars, Stephanie asked, "What are you going to do? Are you going back to your job?"

"No, I'm staying here. I only had a few more days, and the company is aware of Dad's sudden death. They don't expect me to come back. I don't really know about school yet. Mom's going to need some help with the business. I need time to think about everything and talk it all over with her."

"Well, in any case, you should get that thumb looked at first thing tomorrow. You don't want it to get infected."

"Yeah, and it really hurts. I'll call Dr. Blake in the morning."

As Stephanie drove off, Will walked back inside to find his mother and Erin sitting together on the couch. Johanna was telling Erin about their work with Sam, setting up the business and the writing of the will.

"We wanted to ensure a succession of the farm property and the fabrication business if something were to happen to him, or me. Even though I'm the primary beneficiary of your dad's will, his wish was to pass on both the farm and business to the next generation. You both know we started building a family farmhouse out there. Just last night we talked about going out there this week to check on the progress.... Anyway, there's a provision in the will for each of you to own shares."

"Is there anything in Dad's will about his preference for a funeral service? Did you ever purchase cemetery plots?" Erin asked.

"No, he didn't say anything about a funeral. Like I said, we always put that subject off for another day."

Johanna crushed out the cigarette in an ashtray with a thoughtful expression then said, "Now that I think about it, though, right after your grandfather died and Lew inherited the farm, he mentioned a preference to be cremated. I'm going to follow his wish so I hope you kids are okay with it."

She had barely gotten the words out when her body shook with sobs of grief. "Dammit, Lew, why weren't you more careful? Look what you've done."

Erin knelt beside Johanna's chair and put her arm around her mother. "It's okay, Mom; you know Dad wasn't one to take chances. It was just an accident. Nobody's fault."

Will sensed the exhaustion of a tough day from all of them. "Mom, you need to get some rest. It's been a hard day for all of us, especially you. We can talk more tomorrow. Erin, if you can find some sheets for the sleeper sofa, I'll sleep in here."

Erin grabbed a bottle of pills from the kitchen counter and followed her mother toward the bedroom. "Dr. Blake prescribed these sleeping pills for Mom. I'll bring you the sheets after I give these to her."

Will unfolded the sleeper sofa wondering how his life would change in the days and weeks ahead.

Chapter 8

Will swallowed three aspirin before bed and another three at 2 a.m. for the persistent pain in his swollen left thumb, and tried to sleep with it wrapped in a bag of crushed ice. Lack of sleep from physical and emotional pain left him exhausted in the morning.

He called Dr. Blake's office at their opening hour. The nurse directed him to the emergency room at St. Anthony's hospital. She promised the doctor would call in a prescription for an x-ray and pain medicine.

At St. Anthony's Will signed in at the patient check-in window before finding a seat as far away from the coughing crowd as possible. In about twenty minutes, a nurse led him to an exam cubicle, looked at his sore thumb, and checked his vitals.

His painful wait of several minutes ended when an attractive young woman walked in, held out her hand, and said, "Good morning. I'm Dr. Singletary."

Will stood to introduce himself and shook her hand while reading *Dr. Cynthia Singletary* on her white coat, with *Emergency Service, Resident* printed beneath her name.

"I understand you hurt your thumb. Let's take a look."

He took in her blue eyes and blond hair as he lifted his left hand. Her milk-white skin and soft waving hair allowed him to ignore the pain until her soft hands moved his thumb. Grimacing, he explained the previous day's accident.

She said, "I think we can relieve your pain by reducing the swelling and pressure. We'll give you something to numb it and then we'll bleed off the captured blood that's swelling it up and creating the pressure and pain. After that we can get an x-ray to determine the damage. I'll go get the nurse to give you a local anesthesia."

The nurse came in with a small syringe and inserted it into the base of his thumb. In moments, the pain subsided. She left and minutes later Dr. Singletary returned with what looked like a small soldering gun.

"This device will burn through the thumbnail to drain some blood, which will reduce the swelling and pain. Is your thumb numb?" She grinned.

He returned her smile and echoed an answer. "Yep, I have a numb thumb."

She took his hand with her left hand and, holding the look-alike soldering gun with her right, touched the hot tip to his nail. In seconds it burned through, releasing a small stream of blood. He immediately noticed a reduction in the pressure and swelling.

After they took an x-ray, Dr. Singletary returned to report no major damage, only small cracks in the bone. She brought out a hand brace.

Still entranced by her blue eyes and flawless complexion, Will struggled to absorb her words. She had to be at least a couple of years older, but that didn't bother him. He couldn't take his eyes off her.

She cradled his hand, sliding and wrapping the brace in place. That's when he noticed the engagement ring. His excitement faded fast. *Well, damn, she's taken.*

Before he left the hospital, he found a phone and called his mother. He knew there were unfinished jobs in the shop, particularly the Kerr-McGee job, which required attention despite his father's death. Customers needing products wouldn't wait for mourning, and Will wanted to know if she had talked to Paul Smith, their longtime shop supervisor.

"Yes," she replied on the phone. "I called Paul at home early this morning. He was shocked, of course, and took the news hard. You know, he was the first man Lew hired when we started the business and the one person Lew depended on to keep the shop running smoothly. Anyway, he assured me he'd do whatever is necessary to keep the projects on schedule, and I'm sure he knows who to call to get some extra time to repair the paint problem on the Kerr-McGee job."

"Good," Will said. "They bandaged my thumb and put on a brace. I'm leaving the hospital now, and will go directly to the shop and talk to Paul. I'll come by later to check on you."

He found Paul outside the shop office, in front of the Kerr-McGee project. Will was sure Paul was knowledgeable of the project schedule and wondered if he had contacted the client for a few extra days to fix the paint issue.

"Good morning, Paul. The separator looks good. I see you're working on that paint issue. I expect it won't be shipping today?"

"Good morning, Will. No, but we'll be ready to load it by Wednesday," Paul replied. He removed his hat as his eyes filled with tears. Shaking Will's hand, he said, "I'm so sorry about your dad. All of us here in the shop feel bad that the paint flaw caused his accident. We've cleaned, sanded, and primed the flawed areas and should have the final coat of paint on tomorrow. Kerr-McGee has given us a couple of days extra on the shipping date."

"Thanks, Paul," Will said. "The accident wasn't your fault, or anyone else's. It was just an accident, hard as that is for all of us to accept. Is there anything I can do to help you? OU classes start in two weeks, but until then, I'm at your service."

"Thanks, Will, I appreciate your offer. What happened to your hand?"

"I smashed my thumb on the oil rig yesterday. No major damage, but it'll limit my manual labor abilities for a few days."

"There is something you might help with while we're getting the Kerr-McGee job finished. Your father was planning to visit a Phillips Petroleum production well they're shutting in to look at the process unit and storage tanks. It's a typical source of our salvage and rework business. Your dad was good at recognizing process vessels and tanks that could be refurbished and resold. You can meet the production manager, check to see if the units are in good condition, and make an offer. I can coach you on what to look for and options on what to offer, if you're willing to go check it out."

"Sure. Tell me what I need to know, and I'll do it. It'll give me some firsthand knowledge of how this all works."

"We usually offer 10 or 15 percent over scrap value, depending on the condition of equipment. I'll give you a list of the tanks and vessels we look for and relative value. Make a reasonable offer and hold to it. Phillip's only alternative in this down economy is to scrap them."

The need, or opportunity, to fill his father's role broadened Will's thoughts. *Someone has to fill Dad's shoes. If it's going to be me, this could be the start of learning the skills I'll need.*

Paul made the call to the Phillip's regional office to make an appointment for an on-site meeting the next afternoon. He showed Will the information he had on the separator and tanks, including their relative value by size or capacity.

Will left early the next morning and met Bill Renfro, the Phillips production manager, before noon. Bill knew Lew from previous deals, and he expressed his condolences and welcomed Will. They walked the well site inspecting the separator and tanks for sale. Will pulled a spiral notebook with the information Paul had given him and, after making a few notes of his own, made an offer.

Bill asked for more. "I expected a little better price. These tanks aren't junk. They were new a year ago and are still in excellent condition. With some cleaning and a fresh coat of paint, you could easily resell them."

"Except, we also have to break down the piping, load it all onto trailers, and make at least two trips to our yard. Then clean, repaint, and store them until we can find an independent operator that can use this particular size equipment. The market for rebuilt tanks is slow. My offer is approximately 15 percent above scrap value before we add refurbishing costs. We'll do well if we can recover our costs and make a few bucks."

Suddenly, their conversation was interrupted by a loud pickup driving onto the site, kicking up hot dust and loose gravel. It slid to a stop next to the Phillips company car. A middle-aged man in bib overalls and a straw hat stepped out of an early-1950s truck and approached Bill.

"Are you with Phillips Petroleum?"

"I am, sir. What can I do for you?" Bill answered.

"You could turn my gas back on."

"And you are?"

"Ruggles, Joe Dan Ruggles. I own this land. That's my house over there." He pointed to an aging ranch-style farmhouse about a quarter of a mile away. "You're new out here, ain't you?"

"I'm Bill Renfro, in charge of capping this well and clearing the site." While the landowner shook his hand, Bill turned to introduce Will. "This is Will McCall. He's talking with us about purchasing some of this equipment that we'll remove. You should have received a letter explaining the shutdown due to low production and a drop in the price of crude oil. The cost of hauling produced water was more than the sale of the oil, losing money for Phillips—and the investors, like you."

"I got a letter but I didn't know you were gonna shut off my gas. I own the minerals rights and the other Phillips guy said I could keep takin' natural gas as long as it's flowing."

"Well, let's look." Bill turned to lead the group to the large oil and gas separator. They passed the wellhead piping sticking out of the ground with large valves and flanges closely connected.

"I'm guessing nobody ever explained this oil production business to you?" Bill said.

"No, I just signed the papers for my minerals royalty and later they asked if I wanted some natural gas. We said, sure, if we can use it instead of paying the utility for it."

"This is the wellhead, the source of the oil and natural gas, and over here is where we separate the two and any water that's mixed in with the oil. The mixture is why it's called crude oil. The separated oil and water go to those large storage tanks." He glanced at Will. "Mr. McCall is probably going to take this unit and the tanks off our hands."

Will nodded, then Bill continued. "The oil is sold, and the water's hauled to a disposal well. This well doesn't make enough gas to sell; that's why it's been available to you. Now that we're shutting the well and capping the oil, we'll connect the gas from the wellhead to the pipe running to your house. Have you been getting enough gas for use at your house?"

"Well, yes. Until there wasn't any," Mr. Ruggles said. "We realized they shut it off when we ran out of hot water. This gas fuels our furnace in winter and the hot water tank all year, so we don't have to buy gas. We use the meter at the house to estimate how much we saved each month. My wife puts that amount in a kitchen jar. She calls it her gas money. I call it her mad money, 'cause if she can't save it, she gets mad."

Bill chuckled. "I understand. I'll have a man out here tomorrow to get your gas back on. Sorry for the interruption."

"Thanks, I sure appreciate it. Thanks for explaining how this all works." They shook hands and Mr. Ruggles got back in the old pickup, waving as he drove away.

Will and Bill continued walking around the site, doing their inspections. Finally Bill said, "I think we're done. You've got a deal. Your price is above scrap and we don't have any better choices." Bill continued pointing out details regarding safety precautions related to unhooking the tanks and piping.

Will was still curious about the small gas line. "Tell me about Mr. Ruggles's gas line running to his farmhouse. If it's still flowing natural gas from the oil reservoir, isn't the pressure too high for domestic use? And don't you usually burn off the gas before producing the oil?"

"Yes, we do burn off the gas at time of completion because it's not worth the cost of constructing a gas line to a remote sales point. Right now, natural gas at the wellhead is selling for about one dollar per thousand cubic feet, so it's not commercially viable unless it's a big reservoir of gas and a sales line is close by."

He paused and looked toward the house in the distance before continuing. "For the landowner, this gas has a higher heating value than the pure methane sold by the utility. We put a pressure regulator here and another one on the meter at his house, to reduce the pressure for residential use at his furnace and hot water tank. If it continues to flow, he'll get free natural gas for months, maybe even years, saving them a few hundred dollars every year."

"Okay, we'll be careful not to disturb that new line," Will answered.

They shook hands and Will climbed back into his father's Ford pickup and turned onto the county road heading home. He'd gained a measure of confidence from this firsthand experience and felt better about possibly stepping into his dad's job. His mechanical engineering skills could wait for now.

Maybe this won't be a burden after all. Maybe it's an opportunity.

Chapter 9

They held a memorial service for William Lewis McCall the following Saturday at the Lutheran church less than a mile from the McCall's home and business. Lew and Johanna made a monthly pledge and attended church regularly. Johanna had Lew's body cremated and interred in the church's columbarium. The service ended in the columbarium courtyard, with Lew's urn placed in one of the two niches Johanna had purchased a few days earlier.

They held a reception in the parish hall after the service. Friends, family, and current and former business colleagues attended and were gracious in their condolences and best wishes for the McCall family.

Sam Buchanan pulled Johanna aside. "I've petitioned the probate court to validate and release Lew's will to you as executrix and representative of his estate. I know you have a copy and are aware of the contents, but I assume your children don't know the details."

"You're right; they know he had a will but not the terms of it."

"Since they're all beneficiaries, I'll send a copy to each of them when it's released by the court. I'll be available to meet with any or all of you to answer questions. I believe you're the beneficiary of his life insurance and the joint owner of other properties. Those will stay in your name without question or probate court review. In the meantime, call me if you have questions or need anything."

"Thank you, Sam. I appreciate your help, as always. I'll tell the kids you'll be sending them a copy of Lew's will. I expect we'll want to meet with you at some point. I'll let you know when we can all get together."

Many of the guests had left the reception when Stephanie approached her mother. "I'm leaving. We need to relieve the babysitter."

"Of course, I understand. I just talked to Sam about your father's will. You'll get a copy after the probate court approves it. I'll be the executor to carry out its terms, and I want you to know your father left equal shares of his half ownership in the company to each of you. Sam will assist me and can help answer your questions."

"That's interesting. I expect I'll have questions, but I haven't had time to think about it yet. I need to go. I'll talk to you later."

"Okay. I'm going to tell Will and Erin. I'll call you soon about a date that will work for all of us to meet with Sam."

Upon hearing the information, Erin said, "That's a surprise. I'm interested to know more."

"Really?" Will asked. "We'll each own part of the company? I assumed you'd be the sole owner since you formed the company as a partnership, each the beneficiary of the other in case of death. Not right?"

"No," his mother answered. "The charter of the partnership stipulates that shares owned by us individually cannot be sold, transferred, or given to anyone outside the family. I planned to write a similar will, but never did. It was your dad's great desire for the business to stay in the McCall family and for his children to carry on the legacy of family ownership. I'll continue to own 50 percent in partner with you all. We can talk more about it at the meeting with Sam so he can answer your questions and explain it in detail."

They each received their copy of Lew's will about a week later, and everyone agreed to a meeting with Sam at five o'clock the following Monday at Sam's office in the Bank of Oklahoma Tower.

Chapter 10

Sam's assistant, Mary, greeted Will, Johanna, and Erin at the large glass entrance doors of Brown Buchanan, Attorneys at Law, and led them into a conference room with a long, polished walnut table surrounded by executive leather chairs. They chose chairs next to one another along one side and declined Mary's offer of coffee, instead reaching for a pitcher of water and glasses sitting on the table.

"Hello, everyone." Sam's eyes scanned the room. "We're missing one, aren't we?"

"I expect Stephanie soon," Johanna said. "I imagine her husband was late getting home to babysit."

"Sure," Sam answered. "Mary, would you watch for her at the front and show her in when she gets here?"

He closed the door and took a seat. "While we wait for Stephanie, let me say that while your mother will execute the wishes of your father as stated in his will, I'm here to support her, and all of you, and to answer questions or assist as needed."

Sam opened a leather portfolio and pulled out a legal-size file folder. He explained Johanna's responsibility to carry out Lew's wishes, including distribution of property or monies as directed, the liquidation of assets if appropriate, distributing the proceeds, and paying any taxes owed. As he concluded, Mary escorted Stephanie into the room.

"Sorry I'm late." Stephanie rolled out a leather chair next to Erin.

"Welcome, Stephanie. I'm glad you could join us," Sam replied. "I know it's hard to get away when you have small children. I've explained to the others your mother's responsibilities in carrying out your father's wishes expressed in his will, and that I will give her any support she needs. Do you have questions on that subject?"

"Not right now. Please go on, and thanks for your help through this difficult time."

"Each of you should have received your copy of the will and I assume you've had time to look it over. Unless there are any questions, I'll go ahead with a summary of your father's wishes."

When no questions arose, Sam continued reviewing the properties jointly owned with Johanna: the family trailer house, the business property, and the house under construction in Grady County. All would stay with her. Sam confirmed Johanna as the primary beneficiary of all Lew's insurance benefits and personal property, then moved on to the ownership of the company.

"Your father's directive is different regarding his shares of McCall's Production Equipment Company. We chartered the company as a partnership owned equally by William Lewis and Johanna McCall. Lew's will directs his 50 percent ownership to be divided equally among each of his three children."

Stephanie, Will, and Erin glanced at each other with wide eyes and scrambled to find the page of the will describing what Sam said.

Sam continued, "It was Lew's desire that one or more of his children take an active part in the business. The ownership share of the business inherited by a minor child would be held in trust until they are twenty-one years of age. That clause affects only Erin, who just turned nineteen."

Stephanie was first to raise her hand with a question. "So, what does all that mean? What does my inherited one-third share mean in terms of dollars?"

Will corrected her. "It's actually one-third of one-half, or one-sixth, ownership."

She scowled at him and snapped, "I was asking Sam."

"I should have been more precise," Sam answered. "Allow me to elaborate. Your brother is correct, but there's more to it. First, we must determine the current value of the company, which is an appraisal process that will take time. I've recommended an appraisal firm familiar with oil field equipment to your mother."

Johanna nodded.

Sam continued. "When that's completed, we'll know the value of your ownership. For sale or transfer of ownership purposes, the valuation will be unchanged for five years, and the company charter stipulates ownership must stay in the family. So, you can only sell, transfer, or gift your shares to another family member. After five years, if a family member wants to transfer shares, the company would be revalued."

"Oh, great!" Stephanie said curtly. "You mean my shares are worthless unless Mom or Will wants to buy them. Right?"

"And not worth anything to me for another two years," Erin grumbled under her breath.

"Just what is the problem here?" Johanna's voice conveyed both hurt and anger. "Your father's giving you part ownership of the family business, a thriving business we built through hard work and sacrifice, and you act like it's a worn-out hand-me-down. A burden, instead of a gift of considerable value. Is any one of you grateful for this gift, willing to get involved, help it grow in value?"

"Mom, I think we could all use a little more time to absorb all this," Will said. "Time to understand what it means to each of us. I'm sorry, but you know none of us, including me, were planning on working in the business, and I'm not sure ownership changes that."

"If any of you don't want your father's gift, we can fold your shares back into the company treasury. Maybe I'll just buy them myself."

Stephanie didn't hesitate to air her true feelings. "You don't need to speak for me, Will. Charley and I will run our own oilfield service business someday. We've discussed McCall's Production and Equipment and decided cleaning oil storage tanks and reselling them is not our idea of an exciting business, let alone a way to make a comfortable living."

She avoided her mother's glare as she continued. "Whatever business we decide on, we'll need cash to get it started. I was expecting to receive some money from the inheritance, but that's not what I'm hearing, unless one of you wants to buy my ownership. I'm happy to accept Dad's gift, but I'm here to tell you, it's for sale whenever the company stock has a monetary value."

"Mom, we need to hear from you," Will said. "What help are you going to need to keep the business going without Dad? You've been the administrative backbone of the company, managing the payroll, paying bills, doing taxes—all those internal duties required to keep the company together. But Dad was the only one who knew how to buy and sell salvage equipment. He was sales manager, purchasing manager, and head of manufacturing all in one. So, regardless of our partnership, you're going to need someone to fill Dad's shoes, and soon!"

"If there are no more questions for me," Sam said. "I'll excuse myself and let you all continue the family meeting. Johanna, we'll talk again after we get the company valuation report. In the meantime, let me know if I can help."

"Why don't we continue our meeting over dinner," Johanna said. "I arranged this time with a family dinner in mind. It's a good chance to discuss your father's will and the ownership he's giving each of you. Steph, I'd like to hear more about your concerns."

"I'm sorry, Mom, I can't. I've got to get back. I ate before I came, and Charley doesn't do babysitting well. He'll be mad if I'm out too long. I'll call you later."

Will and Erin said in unison, "Sounds good." Will added, "If you're buying."

"I'm thinking of a juicy steak." Johanna said. "How 'bout Cattleman's Steakhouse, your father's favorite. Expensive, but we're worth it, don't you think?"

<><><>

Johanna led Will and Erin into the steakhouse, where they were ushered to a plush leather-cushioned booth. Erin excused herself to find the restroom. "Order me a glass of iced tea and a cheeseburger with everything on it. I'll be right back."

The waitress appeared right away with menus. She took their drink orders, then explained an expensive surf and turf special before leaving to get the drinks.

Will spoke immediately. "Mom, this week has given me a chance to review my plans, and I need your input before making some decisions."

"There's no need for you to change your plans," Johanna responded quickly. "Finishing at OU, getting your Petroleum Engineering degree, is all you need to focus on. Besides, if you drop out of school, you'll be subject to the draft. The war in Vietnam is pulling in more and more young men. You're almost through and I know your father would want you to finish, get your degree. Getting drafted doesn't help me and could ruin your career goals."

"You don't have to worry about the draft. Last year, the Selective Service changed the draft to a lottery system. This year's draft will draw from men born in 1951 and later. Since I was born in '48, I'm safe for the near future, and hopefully President Nixon will end this stupid war soon."

"Well, that's good." Relief filled her. "But it doesn't change my thinking about the business while you finish at OU. Right now, with the slow economy, we're not financially able to hire anyone. I'll manage the office and finances of the business and Paul Smith can take on more responsibility for sales and manufacturing until you graduate. Paul has worked with your father since we started the business. He knows the restoration process and most of the customers. Meanwhile, you can help Paul and me review and discuss a long-range business plan."

"Okay, but you need to be honest about whether the company could support a new operations manager. I'd be almost no help part-time. Maybe Paul could be the operations manager and someone else in the shop could step up as shop supervisor."

"Now, that's another possibility I hadn't thought of. You're making my case for you staying in school."

"Dad's will spoke of his vision for the future, and he didn't expect you to run this company all by yourself. I've got a lot to learn, but I spent a day in Dad's shoes last week negotiating the purchase of a separator and storage tanks. Paul coached me and I made a good buy. I can do the job and start tomorrow. With help from Paul and you, I think I can contribute positively in a month or two."

Johanna opened her mouth to speak, and Will held up his hand to stop her, then leaned forward. "You're already working sixty hours a week doing an outstanding job as CFO, purchasing manager, and office manager. Taking on more would be impossible. I've thought about it since the accident, and I believe we can do it together. I have some engineering skills and this summer has taught me a lot about how this oil and gas business works, how the people think and act."

He sat back again. "Stephanie is busy with her own family and Erin is in school. My life is still an open book with no other responsibilities. Dad's expressed desire to keep the business in the family speaks to me. If he could talk to us now, I think he'd agree with me."

"That's a wonderful offer and I love you for wanting to help me, and the business." She paused for a moment then added, "Take the next few days to think this through before you have to leave for school, and I will too."

Johanna spoke those words while holding back her deep-down desire for him to join the company. The thought of working with her son was already quenching the burning pain of her husband's sudden death. His engineering education and energy could move the company into new production equipment with real growth potential.

"Another thing, while you're thinking this through," she continued, "dropping out before getting your degree could be a big mistake. If the company gets into financial trouble or just doesn't survive, it'll be difficult to get a good job. You might have to go back to school to finish your degree, and that would be harder after being away."

Erin slid into the booth beside her mother during the last remark. She looked across at Will. "What? Are you thinking of quitting school and going to work with Mom?"

"We were discussing the possibility. Mom's going to need someone to fill Dad's shoes, a man with experience working with production equipment. Unfortunately, even if we found someone with that experience, I doubt the business could afford him."

He twirled a salt shaker, then continued. "Of course, I don't have Dad's experience, contacts, or knowledge of the market. So it won't be easy. But I can learn. For a while, I'll be little more than a go-fer, but eventually, I'll contribute and earn my keep."

"Sounds like you're committed to making it work," Erin said. "That's encouraging. I only have one choice: go on to college."

Johanna spoke up. "As Will said, we're talking; but I want him to take some time to consider all options, the pros and cons. Dropping out of college with only two semesters remaining could be a big mistake. You sleep on it, son, and we'll talk again."

Chapter 11

Will's technical skills could be useful someday, but he knew he lacked the day-to-day knowledge of buying and selling used equipment needed to step into his father's shoes. The marketing skills necessary today would take time to learn. Assessing the value of used equipment and restoration costs is a skill gained from years of hands-on experience.

But who else was there?

The next week he was driving back from lunch agonizing over dropping out of his senior year at OU, not getting his diploma. Without that piece of paper, he'd never be able to secure a genuine job as a professional engineer. But the advanced mechanical engineering courses he'd take in his final year wouldn't be of any help in running the family salvage equipment business.

The long-sought goal of working as a professional engineer would have to wait.

Will parked his Bronco beside the office trailer, sitting there for a moment, organizing his thoughts before telling his mother of his decision.

She also needs some help to get the house construction back on schedule. I'll offer to contact the builder to get an update and see if there are construction holds waiting on her.

He went inside and back to her office. A half-eaten tuna sandwich and a glass of iced tea were on the corner of her desk next to the ashtray holding a burning Marlboro. Johanna was making entries in a ledger.

Will knocked on the wall. "Mom, do you have time to talk?"

She looked up with a smile. "Of course, son. Did you have lunch?"

"Yes, and a quiet one for a change. The appraisers are due in about an hour. Are you ready to meet with them?"

"Yes, I just have to finish adding a couple of entries to update a ledger of projects and sales for the last twelve months. Paul has agreed to give them a tour of the shop."

"Good. I came to explain my decision to join the company. I want to go to work with you. I've thought of all the options, pros, and cons, and this is the best for both of us. Sure, I won't get a degree in mechanical engineering, but, as my new employer," he winked, "I doubt you'll require one. The lack of a degree doesn't mean I'm not a good engineer, and someday I can use my education and engineering knowledge to help this company move out of the salvage business into manufacturing. In the meantime, I can use that vision to motivate me as I work long hours with you learning this business. Does that make sense?"

She stood, walked around her desk, and hugged him as she said, "If it makes sense to you, motivates you, and you're sure, you have my blessing and support. The thought of working with you is already easing the pain from the loss of your father. I know you can do it. I just wanted you to be sure it's what you want, not because you feel obligated."

"Thanks, Mom. I know we need to come up with some type of work schedule, and I'd like to talk about what I can do that will help you and Paul keep things moving. I'll work on some ideas, then let's all three of us take an hour or two to hash out how I can best get into the workflow around here."

"Sounds good." She moved back toward the ledger and picked up her pencil, but turned back to Will when he spoke again.

"I also want to help you finish your new house. You still plan to move into it when it's finished, don't you? Meanwhile, if it's okay with you, I'd like to move home with you now that Erin is away at school. Is that all right?"

His mother's shoulders dropped and her expression sagged. "Of course you can. But I can't bring myself to deal with the final construction without your father. It'll take some time to accept it as just my home now, not ours."

"What's the current completion schedule, and what about financing?"

"You dad's life insurance is enough to pay off the house with some left over. Even though it might be smarter, for tax reasons, to continue the mortgage, since I have the money I'd sleep better knowing I owned the house free and clear."

"Why don't I call the builder to get an updated schedule? I can meet with him or his crew to see what we need to do to move the work along. You can choose how much and when you want to get involved."

Will began spending seven days a week learning

the financial side of the family business from his mother and taking a hands-on approach to learning the shop restoration processes. He was also thinking about the future. How he could apply his engineering education to the manufacturing of new production equipment? This had to be the company's future, but how, when, and at what cost?

He spent what spare time he had helping his mother with the decisions necessary to get the new house finished. In a few weeks, the exterior was complete except for landscaping. Finally, carpets and appliances were in. Two weeks before Thanksgiving, she moved in.

Chapter 12

November 1969

Johanna picked up the ringing phone and exchanged greetings with Sam Buchanan.

"I called to let you know I've received the appraisal of the company's valuation," he said. "Would you and Will have time today or tomorrow to go over the results? And, of course, we can include your girls if they're interested and available."

"Will and I will meet with you, and I'll tell Steph and Erin you've received the report and will send them a copy. They can contact you, or me, if they have questions."

"I can come to your office this afternoon if it's convenient," Sam said.

"That should work. It's an unusually quiet Friday. We don't have a job we're trying to get out the door. How about two o'clock?"

Sam agreed and Johanna replied, "Good. I'll let Will know, and we'll see you then."

Sam arrived as promised, and Johanna directed him to a small, round conference table. "Will should be here soon. Can I get you anything? Coffee, or water?"

"No, thank you, Johanna. I had a late lunch. How are you doing? How's the new home coming along?"

"I moved in last week. Will's been helping me finish the details and getting me moved. I had a tough time finishing it without Lew. He would've loved to help me with last-minute changes and fill the garage with tools he always wanted. Now I'm dealing with being alone. When something comes up, good or bad, without thinking I still reach for the phone to call him."

Will knocked, then entered. "Good afternoon, Sam. It's good to see you again. I understand you've received the valuation report. We're eager to hear the results."

He took a chair next to his mother at the round table as Sam handed each of them a copy of the report and explained, "There are several methods to determine the market value of a company. We define the value of a public company as the price of their stock listed on an exchange, such as the New York Stock Exchange. We calculate the value of privately owned companies by their assets and earnings, weighted according to their strength and whether it's a service business or a manufacturer. In the case of a closely held private company such as yours, an independent appraiser looks at hard assets and earnings, including future earnings, plus other factors such as performance compared to competitors to arrive at a market value."

"I expect in today's economic environment our earnings are low, which suggests to me the company share value will be low," Will replied.

"True," Sam agreed. "It's not a strong economic time, but I think you'll all be happy with the results. The first section explains the process in more legal detail than you may want. So let's go the the numbers on page five. The appraiser's bottom line shows a total valuation of $152,700. That figure includes last year's annual net earnings of $25,500 and the net assets of $85,360."

Sam paused and glanced around the table before continuing. "The total includes other factors the appraiser details in the report to arrive at a total market valuation. McCall's Production Equipment Company was established as an S corporation with two shareholders each holding 100 shares. This valuation establishes the individual share value of $763.50. So Lew's 100 shares and Johanna's 100 shares are worth $76,350."

Johanna did the math. "So Lew's 50 percent ownership is divided by three, giving each of the children ownership at $25,450, or 33.33 shares each."

"Yes," Sam said. "You and your children can use this document as the basis for selling or trading ownership. I can draw up the papers to reflect this valuation and we'll show the share ownership of each member of the family. I'll send copies of this to Erin and Stephanie, and you'll all have a document detailing the number of shares owned by each person."

Sam said, "Yes, that works out well. I'll draw up the papers to reflect this valuation, as well as the ownership share of each member of the family. I'll send copies of this to Erin and Stephanie, and later you'll all get a document detailing the number of shares owned by each."

"Thank you, Sam, for putting this together. I see you've attached an invoice covering the work. I'll get a check in the mail to you next week."

"Nothing's really changed, but it feels good to have that done, anyway," Johanna said after Sam left.

"I agree. And I think the girls will be happy to know the monetary value of their shares that they can use to sell or trade shares in the future."

After work that evening, Johanna called Erin at Oklahoma Christian College and Stephanie at home to give them the good news.

Stephanie said, "If you or Will want to buy my shares, let me know."

Erin said, "Save it for me, Mom. Someday I might better appreciate Dad's gift. Right now, I see only two things in my future, college and Phil."

Chapter 13

Stephanie sat next to Charley and stared at the television screen, but her mind focused, as usual, on money. She thought she'd inherit some money when her dad died, which she could use to save her from a life of bad choices and living paycheck to paycheck. But that didn't happen. She had to find a path to a better life.

It was Sunday, the only day Charley didn't haul wastewater. They ate dinner early on TV trays watching the football game. Stephanie picked up the plates and trays but wasn't in the mood to do dishes. When the game was over Charley reached for the newspaper, but Stephanie stopped his hand.

"Charley, I know you don't want to work for your father all your life, so let's figure out how we can work for ourselves. Your father will work you to death if you let him. He treats you like any employee, not like his son. I know you try to satisfy his every demand, thinking he'll cut you some slack or give you a bonus. Let's be realistic. As long as you jump when he says jump, he'll keep pushing you to do more."

"Yeah, so how do we break out of the rut?" Charley barked back.

"I'm thinking about the business ownership I inherited from Dad. So far, it's only been worth the paper it's printed on, but yesterday I got a report from the attorney with the true value of the company and what my ownership is worth."

"And? How much is your cut worth?"

"It says I own 2,545 shares of the company, and each share is worth $10."

"Really? So you could sell you part and get over $25,000."

"I wish. The way Dad set it up, I can only sell my share to another family member. None of them but Mom could afford to buy it, and she won't. At least, not now."

"So it's just as worthless as ever."

"No, I have an idea. I'm thinking we use this stock as collateral to borrow the down payment for our own water truck. Maybe even two. Hire another driver and haul twice as much."

Charley looked more interested in her idea than she'd seen him about anything in a long time. "Now, that's an idea with genuine possibilities," he said. "Do we have to form a company? How do we do that?"

"No idea, but I bet Sam Buchanan—Mom's attorney—could help us out, or maybe get us the proper paperwork so we can do it ourselves. I'll call him tomorrow. Why don't you call your father and ask him to co-sign a loan for us to buy a truck? Just in case the bank won't loan against my company shares. We need to get this going as soon as possible."

"Hmm." Charley looked thoughtful. "We can't use my name for the business, since Dad's already using our last name."

"I'm thinking we can call it C&S Services. Get it? We'll be partners; you do the hauling, and I'll do the office work."

As soon as Charley stepped in the door after work the next day, Stephanie said, "Did you ask JD about helping us with a loan?"

"Yeah, I asked him. At first he blew me off. Said we could never do it, 'cause we don't know anything about running a business. We argued about it, and I left."

Stephanie opened her mouth but Charley interrupted her to continue as he sat down. "I went back later and proposed that we use the new truck to keep hauling his wastewater while we try to get our own customers established. He agreed, on the condition that we hire and train a driver to use our truck and I keep driving the Arnold Oil and Gas truck. I said it was a deal, and he told me about somebody who has a truck for sale. Then he agreed to meet at the bank to co-sign for the loan."

"See, I knew you could do it." Stephanie bent down to wrap her arms around him and gave him a big kiss. "You stood your ground and made a sensible proposal he couldn't resist. I have an appointment with an attorney who'll help us put together C&S Trucking Services Company. When we hire another driver, we'll be able to provide water hauling service for our company with either truck."

Soon the new C&S Trucking Services Company was in business. Charley continued to drive for his father part-time, resulting in a heavy work schedule.

Within a few months, C&S added a gin-pole truck equipped with winches and poles for lifting and hauling heavy equipment. Business slowly picked up, but loan payments and costs reduced profits of the new company.

The revenue covered only the bank loan, expenses, and the grocery bill.

Despite the work load, Stephanie went to visit her mother almost every day. She and Crystal even stayed overnight with her several times when Charley worked late or was out of town. The activity and sounds of her daughter and granddaughter in the house seemed to lift Johanna's spirit.

One day Charley called her at Johanna's and suggested they go out to dinner.

"What? We don't have extra money to spend going out to dinner."

"Hon, we'll just get a burger. Ask your mom if she'll watch Crystal, and I'll pick you up in about an hour."

Stephanie hesitated but then replied, "All right. Yes! I'll see you in an hour."

She was still waiting at six fifteen. It was rare for them to have a chance to get away together, if just an hour for burgers. *What could be so important he'd ditch me for it? Or did he just forget about me?*

Honk!

Moments later they were riding in Charley's Ford Power Stroke diesel pickup with chrome bumpers and oversized aluminum wheels, headed for Pennington's Drive-In in South Oklahoma City. After ordering two cheeseburgers in a basket with fries and two chocolate shakes, he said, "I've discovered how we can make some real money hauling water."

"You mean there really is money to be made hauling water? I give up. What's the secret we've been missing?"

"You laugh, but I'll tell you how. We've always been told not to drain the water storage tanks dry. I never thought about it or wondered why. Yesterday, my mind was on other jobs we're working and I accidentally emptied a tank all the way. It was late, so I didn't go to the disposal well but just parked the truck in the yard. This morning I was unloading the water and—you won't believe it—*oil* flowed out."

"Oil? Are you sure? How much? What happened?"

"It was a eureka moment. There's oil in them water tanks! Not barrels, but gallons. From now on, we're going to be hauling water and oil! A much more profitable business for C&S Trucking Services."

He had her attention. This idea had promise. It just might work. Except...

"Wait a minute. Operators pay us to haul off just their wastewater. Taking the oil is stealing... isn't it?"

Charley grinned ear to ear. "Not if they contracted us to take that water. There's always some oil in the water coming from the well. Operators know that. The crude oil goes through a separator to knock out the gas and water. The design relies on the heavier water to fall to the bottom of the separator tank with the lighter oil sitting on top. It takes time for the lighter oil to separate from the produced water. So, water dropping out at the production separator still has some oil in it."

"You mean, you've been hauling and dumping some oil all this time?"

"Yep. Everybody knows the oil doesn't separate completely, but they don't worry about it because it's not profitable to try to recover every drop. It's more important to get the produced oil into a pipeline or sold as quickly as possible. The little bit of oil left in the water is just ignored. That's why I never thought about it."

"You've sure thought about it now."

Charley's face was lit up like a little boy's at

Christmas. "Yep. The key is to take all the produced water somewhere it can sit for a day or two. Then we drain the wastewater, collect the oil off the top, and sell it. All we need is a couple of storage tanks to let it sit in."

"Now I see where you're going. You want me to ask my brother to get us a couple of good used storage tanks to hold it in while it separates."

"Yep. Maybe we should trade the work truck for another tank truck, so we can haul more water. Plus, the water we're hauling for Dad could also come to our tanks to separate. The key is volume. The more water we haul, the more oil we'll sell. Think you can sweet-talk Will into extending us credit on a couple tanks? I'm sure we could pay him back soon, with the additional money the oil will bring."

"Maybe. Or maybe he'll trade them for some of my company shares. Or, even better, trade all my shares for tanks and some cash. Could be enough to buy another tank truck and keep the work truck."

Stephanie ate cold french fries as she thought. The key to a deal would be to play on Will's desire for a larger share of the company. He was too cash poor to buy her shares outright, but this way they'd both be getting what they wanted. Of course, if he knew how much money she and Charley stood to make, it could be harder to negotiate with him.

"Listen, Charley, don't tell your dad about this, or anyone else. It's an internal C&S business strategy, best kept between you and me. I'll make up a story for Will about the use of the tank if necessary."

Chapter 14

Will was in his office early on Monday when the phone rang.

"Will, it's me Steph. Do you have some time?"

"Good morning, Steph. Anything wrong?"

"No, we're good, but the business has slowed down. How's your business?"

"Slow, as you said. Oilfield services of all types have slowed."

"We want to expand our services, but we need more storage for handling the produced water we haul from production sites. Since there are fewer available water disposal wells, we want to put in some storage of our own as an interim holding point. Would you have some tanks we might use?"

Will was sure their new trucking service had already borrowed money from the bank and JD. How else could they have afforded that fancy truck Charley bought? But if business was slow, they didn't have the cash to buy a refurbished tank. He proceeded as tactfully as he knew how.

"We have one in the shop, and I expect more to come in soon. I've got money invested in the one that's ready now, so I'd need to get some money out of it. I could sell it to you for my cost, but...well, aren't you overextended already? I wouldn't want to put you in a bind."

"You're right. We are. So how about a trade? You know I've always wanted to sell my inherited shares in the company, and you're the one family member who could benefit from owning more shares. Erin can't buy them, and Mom...well, it hurts her feelings to bring it up. If you bought them, it would give you a bigger share of the company. You may need that when Mom retires."

"That's possible. But do you want me to buy all your shares? They're worth more than this tank we're talking about."

"Yes, if possible. It could be a win-win for both of us. You get a larger share of the business, and we get a storage tank and some cash. Interested?"

"Yeah, I'm interested. But it'd be difficult for me to take advantage of your offer without putting myself out on a financial limb. I don't have the resources to make that kind of investment. Let me think about it. Mom and I are getting together later to discuss company financing. I'll mention this; maybe she can help. Can I get back to you in a few days?"

"Of course. Mom's planning for us to go out there Sunday for dinner. Let's talk about it then."

"Okay," Will agreed. "I'll see you then."

He hung up and leaned back to think it over. *This could be the right time and vehicle to work out a buyout deal with Mom, since she's already mentioned me taking over someday. Maybe she would finance me buying Stephanie's stock.*

He didn't know how much his mom had inherited from his dad, counting the land, insurance, and company assets. Other than finishing the new house, she hadn't made any large investments.

He got up and walked the few steps to his mother's open office. She was hovering over a payroll spreadsheet. The ashtray on her desk held a burning cigarette and her coffee cup lay just beyond the spreadsheet.

"Mom, can you take a break so we can talk?"

She reached for the cigarette and replied, "Sure, but make it quick. This payroll needs to be completed today. Is there another production problem? That's just what we don't need right now." She took a long drag on the Marlboro as she waited for his reply.

"No, no problems in the shop. I just talked to Steph. She and Charley are trying to expand their business and need some cash. They've already used all their credit at the bank and with JD."

"And now she's coming to us for money?" Johanna exhaled a stream of smoke and set the Marlboro on the full ashtray.

"No; she proposed a sale of her inherited stock to me. I'd like to buy it to increase my ownership of the company, but I don't have enough cash to swing the deal."

In her most stern and stubborn German voice, Johanna said, "Well, that's between you and her, and maybe your bank. Why come to me?"

"Because you're the one who controls the future of the company. I'm ready to make a long-term commitment to you and this company. To move forward with that commitment, I need your financial help. I want to increase my ownership and share the burden of decision-making and management responsibilities with you. I'm proposing to purchase both Stephanie's and Erin's shares."

Johanna gave him a wide-eyed look. "Have they agreed to this?"

"Steph was the one who approached me to buy her shares. I haven't talked to Erin, but I think she's more interested in marrying Phil and raising a family. I'm sure she has no desire to get into this business."

"You're right about that."

"If you're willing, we can get Sam to draft a loan agreement with all the terms spelled out, including any contingencies we can think of. I could pay back the cost of the additional shares over a period of, say, fifteen years. I'll take out an insurance policy to cover the loan in case of my unexpected death."

"So you want to be half owner." She took another quick draw on her cigarette. "I don't remember how much their shares are worth. How much would this loan be?"

"Together, their shares are worth $ 50,900. If you have the money and can loan it to me without draining your savings, we can ask Sam to write up an agreement and I'll pay you back. I'm not sure how much I can pay back each year, but I trust we can come up with a payment plan."

"If we do this, you and I would share equal responsibilities running the company. We'll need time to work out the specific areas of responsibility. Also, I want to be sure Steph and Erin are happy with what we decide. After all, they are part owners of McCall's Production Equipment."

"Yes, I agree. Again, I don't think either has any interest in joining the company, now or in the future.

Doing this now means taking on a serious debt, but if I wait and we're able to grow the company, it could be a lot more expensive to buy their shares. Steph and Charley need the money now to expand their own service business. She knows you're the best one to finance this deal."

"Let's talk again in a day or so before trying to meet with Sam. He may have some ideas, or identify legal and financial hurdles we haven't thought of."

Will agreed and, with no further discussion, went back to his office and started working on the details. The actual buyout would involve little money up front. He would pay Stephanie for her shares. The money loaned by his mother for Erin's shares could be put into her college fund. He might move the company into new product manufacturing. It was risky, but if he worked hard to maintain profitability, it would pay off in the years to come.

The intercom phone interrupted his thoughts. It was Paul from the shop. "Can you stop by the shop and help me with a last-minute problem on a project about ready to ship?"

Will glanced at his watch. Lunch time. He snatched his Bronco keys from the desk and headed to the shop for a short meeting with Paul.

Fifteen minutes later, with the problem solved, he was on his way to Harden's Deli, a longtime favorite of the McCall family.

Chapter 15

Will fell in line at Harden's, waiting to order his favorite pastrami on rye sandwich. He turned to stare out the window, still thinking about buying the company shares. A tap on his shoulder brought him back to reality. A woman's soft voice from behind him said, "I think you're next."

He looked back at the space between him and the order counter, said, "Oh, sorry," and stepped up to order the pastrami sandwich.

As he moved to the side after ordering, he glanced back to see attractive, and familiar, face. It came to him: the hair, the milk-white complexion—it was Cynthia the ER doctor. The beautiful woman he recognized paid at the counter and stepped toward him to wait for her order. He couldn't resist speaking to her.

"Hi. I'm Will McCall. Do you remember me?"

The young woman seemed startled. "No, I don't think so."

"Dr. Singletary from St. Anthony's, right? You patched my injured thumb." He lifted his left hand. "It's healing fine using the brace you gave me."

She smiled. "Oh, you met my sister Cynthia. She's doing her residency at St. Anthony's. She's the smart one in the family. I'm Christi, just a lowly real estate agent." She offered her hand in greeting.

"Wow," Will answered. "You mean your twin sister, your identical twin sister. You fooled me." He reached out and shook her soft hand, very much like the one that had gotten his attention months ago. "I bet this happens often."

"Not really. We work in such different professions. She went to med school, and I went to business school. We're alike in many respects, but we react much differently to the sight of blood." She gave a big smile. "This is my first time in here, but you ordered so quickly I assume you've been here before."

"Yep. It's an excellent deli, my favorite lunch spot. We have a family business nearby and I try to get here for a sandwich at least a couple times a week."

"That's interesting. What is the family business? I'm in this part of town looking at commercial property for a client who wants to move a small business into this area, and I'm not finding any property that fits their needs."

"Our business is recovering and rebuilding oil production equipment. We're located just a few blocks north of here. I think you'll need to go farther south to find a commercial building lot."

Their orders were up, and they both approached the counter again to retrieve their sandwiches.

"Have you got a minute? Can you join me?" He asked, motioning and moving toward a table for two against the wall, hoping she would agree.

"Sure. It beats eating in the car alone." As they shared education histories and family information, he continued to be attracted to her pleasant personality that matched her smile and stylish, casual outfit.

"Sorry, I can't help you with commercial property," Will said, "but I'm also looking for a condo or small home." He couldn't resist extending the conversation with the little fib. She interested him as much as her twin sister had; and since she had no ring on her left hand, he guessed she was single. Besides, he'd love to move out of the doublewide into his own place.

"I handle commercial property, but I can get you information on residential listings in the area."

"That would be great. I need to get back to the shop. Can we get together again? I'd love to show you our business, and hear more about real estate opportunities. Maybe this weekend?"

"How about this Saturday morning? I have a client meeting but should be free by twelve. I could come by your business around noon if that fits your schedule."

"Noon Saturday is good, and maybe we'll catch lunch again. I'll be there all day. Here's my card. Call me when you get free or headed this way."

"Great. I'll see you Saturday."

He shook her soft hand, excited at the prospect of seeing her again.

On the way back to the shop he thought about how fun that was, almost like a first date. *Christi is definitely beautiful like her sister, but more open, more welcoming.*

Late morning the following Saturday his office phone rang.

"Good morning, Will, it's Christi. I'm calling to say I'm running late, but can be at your office a little after noon. Are you still available?"

"Sure. I'm glad you can come by. I have nothing else planned."

"Great. The rural property I was showing took longer than I expected. It'll take me another thirty to forty minutes to get back to your part of town."

"It's not a problem. I have plenty of time. When you get here, just park next to my Ford Bronco in front of the office. I'll be watching for you."

Christi arrived as promised and parked her Oldsmobile Cutlass next to Will's older Ford Bronco.

Will met her at the door. "Good morning, Christi," he greeted. "I'm glad you could come."

"Sorry I'm a little later than I expected."

He held the door open, offering his hand to help her step up into the trailer office.

"My client is looking for some land, a place in the country, so he can become a gentleman farmer or rancher. When he retires, he plans to build a house and barn out there so he can own a couple of horses and maybe some feeder calves. He thinks he wants a quarter section, but he'll soon realize that's more maintenance and taxes than he wants."

Will led her to his desk. "This is it. Please sit here." He motioned to a chair in front of his desk and set against the trailer wall. "Let me take your coat. I've got a pot of coffee on, or I have a Coke if you'd rather." He moved a couple of steps back to a small refrigerator.

"A Coke sounds great. So, that's your Bronco I parked next to?"

"Yes," he said, walking back to her with a cold bottle of Coke. "It works for me. I need to visit remote well sites and that little truck with 4-wheel drive can go anywhere. And I see you're driving a sporty two-door coupe. I thought real estate agents drove big, comfortable Cadillacs to drive clients around in luxury."

"An unfortunate image we inherited from the residential agents who drive wives around looking for a bigger home, or those from out of town whose husbands are being transferred into the area. I deal in commercial real estate; it doesn't require as much chauffeuring around. Many of my clients want to drive their own car in case they get called away on business."

"So, you're hoping to sell him a business site and a farm?"

"Yes. It's an unusual opportunity. I found the client a larger warehouse to lease in a new industrial zone between here and Moore. Now he's looking for an acreage to do some weekend ranching."

"My folks bought this property and started this business about five years ago. They moved from a farm west of here, in Grady County. That's where I grew up, not too far from where you were today. Dad inherited the farm from my grandfather, then sold about half of it to start this business. I know these facilities don't look like much—'low overhead,' as the used car dealers would say—but it works well and it's all paid for. No debt."

"You said you stepped into the business after your father's sudden death. That's admirable. Do you have expansion plans, or do you just want to maintain it, take his place?"

"I dropped out of my senior year at OU to help Mom with the business, since holding it together by herself would have been difficult. Unfortunately, there's not much possibility for growth without expanding into new products." Will paused, but she looked genuinely interested, so he went on.

"Continuing as just a salvage and rework business has a dim future, with limited profit potential or growth in the struggling oil and gas industry. At some point, I'm hoping to design and fabricate new production equipment. I can design the products, but I'm still learning the manufacturing and marketing sides of the business. I'm trying to be realistic about the challenge and take small steps at first. Does that sound reasonable, or too pie in the sky?"

"No, I admire your confidence. I say, go for it."

"Thanks. Come, I'll show you through the shop, then we can get some lunch. I'm hungry."

Chapter 16

1971

After their love-at-first-sight meeting, Will dated Christi for a year. She remained busy selling commercial real estate and he worked long hours learning the McCall's process equipment restoration business. Christi and her mother were finally able to organize a beautiful church wedding, followed by a lavish reception at the Oklahoma City Golf and Country Club.

They both looked forward to raising a family, but after Christi suffered a miscarriage, she started taking the new daily birth control pill. Neither of them wanted to go through that again.

Instead, they devoted their precious spare time to looking for a home for the two of them. Both of them loved the older bungalows built in the '30s with wide front porches. They found it difficult to find a structurally sound older house with good restoration possibility. Some were too expensive to restore and others just too expensive. Will was thrilled when Christi found one in an older neighborhood near downtown. They began restoration, adding modern touches to the original hardwood floors and trim. Will spread the work and costs over several months, so it was another year before they moved in.

One Friday Christi arrived home at six and parked under an extension of the right side of the two-story house that served as a carport. The carport and side entrance protected her from the driving rain brought in by a cold front.

She and Will had planned this Friday night together, a few quiet hours all to themselves. Her weekends were usually busy with clients, and he worked most Saturdays in the shop overseeing the fabrication of new processing units he'd designed. She opened the side door into the kitchen and instantly heard a country and western tune coming from the living room.

She threw her rain jacket on a hook, dropped her satchel on a side chair, and went to the refrigerator for a Coors.

"Sorry I'm late," she hollered from the kitchen. "That song is one of my favorites. If I have a beautiful body, would you hold against me, and if I was dying of thirst would your flowing love quench me? Do you want to answer those questions?"

"What did you say? I'm on the couch in the living room." He shouted back. "Grab a beer and come sit with me."

She came in the living room, turned down the stereo, then walked behind the couch and kissed him on the cheek. "Never mind. Have you ordered the pizza?"

"No, not yet. I was waiting for you."

"So, how's everything at the shop?"

"Good; in fact, incredibly good. We just finished the fabrication of a new gas-oil separator in record time— from quote to completion in less than three weeks. That short turnaround time gives us a competitive edge. The biggest factor is that new computer spreadsheet program we're using. It can generate a design and price estimate in under an hour. That process that used to take hours, sometimes days. That should help ease our cash flow problem."

She had rounded the arm of the couch and slid into his lap, wrapping her free arm around his neck. "When did you become a computer programmer?"

"I'm not, and you probably have more computer skills than me. In my junior year at OU, I took a business course elective. It was about business finances and covered balance sheets and income statements. What I learned in that class was a big help when Dad died. I was able to help Mom with the company books and evaluate the health of the business."

He took a swig of beer before continuing. "The second and more beneficial skill I learned from that course, was the introduction to a new computer software called VisiCalc. You just enter numbers in interactive cells, and the application performs whatever function you ask it to—adding or multiplying, dividing, and lots of other functions. It was designed for accountants but engineers can use it for strength calculations or totaling labor and material costs. It even lets you move columns and combine functions with values in separate cells."

"I see how that can help with bookkeeping, but how does it help you with designing production tanks and high-pressure vessels?"

"First, you determine the size of the vessels. Second, list the materials required. When the cost per unit of all the materials is entered, VisiCalc calculates the total materials costs automatically. Then plug in hours of labor multiplied by labor cost, and add in overhead. The program figures it all, and I've got a price to quote. I can work up a design and estimate while the customer is on the phone."

"Very clever. And you're already using it that way?"

"Yes, but only for a small, straightforward design. I'm working on a template that will allow it to be used even easier and faster. Now, before you tell me about your day, I'm going to call Pizza Hut and have them deliver us a large supreme pizza."

"Deliver it? When did Pizza Hut start bringing pizzas to your house?"

"I don't know. I saw in their newspaper ad today that they offer delivery and thought we'd give it a try."

After calling in their order, Will returned to Christi on the couch.

"Well, smarty pants, I have some special news also," Christie said coyly.

"Oh, yeah? Did you find a computer program that helps you sell more real estate?"

"No. I bought an acreage you know something about."

"You bought some land? Or we did? Or—"

Christi interrupted. "Remember when we first met, I came to your shop on a Saturday morning after showing some land to a client?"

"Yeah, near my mother's property, right?"

"That's the one. The client found something he liked better, and that land sold to someone else."

"And it came up for sale again?"

"No, my father was the someone else. He bought it as an investment and gave me the first right of refusal if he ever decided to sell it. Well, recently he decided to sell, and I exercised my right to buy it from him as an investment. We both loved the land when I originally showed it."

Will was surprised. Maybe even a little hurt. "When were you going to tell me about this?"

"I'm telling you now. This is something my father and I discussed when he bought it, months before we decided to get married. You know it's a long-standing goal of mine to be financially independent, something my parents instilled in me growing up. Plus, I had no idea he'd want to unload the investment now."

"I get it; a single woman making an investment like this is wise, and admirable. But you're not single anymore. What about our marriage and our commitments to be as one? It makes me wonder what else I don't know about you and what else is going on in your family."

Christi scooted closer to him and softly turned his head toward her, eye to eye.

"Will, you know I love you very much. Please believe me. There are no other secrets. And when I pay off the note, I'll put the deed in both our names."

"What are we going to do with it? Do you plan to sell it, or hold it as an investment or until we retire on it?"

"We don't have to decide right now, and the land will appreciate. Land is a good investment, regardless."

"You're right about that. My dad always said land is the best investment you can make. So, tell me more about the property. How many acres, and exactly where is it?"

"It's eighty acres, and it's on the same county road as your mother's property, only about a quarter of a mile west of hers. It has some nice oak trees close to the road and some big cottonwood trees on the north end, alongside a small creek that runs into the Washita River. Plus, there's a house and barn. The house might be the original one built in the early 1900s. I think it's been remodeled more than once but it'll need a lot of TLC."

The property location reminded Will of the McCall family history. "You know, that property may have been part of the original land claim my grandfather made during the Oklahoma Land Run in 1889. Mom's eighty acres may be near or even adjoining that property."

"Maybe I should do a title search to learn the deed history of the land," Christi suggested.

"Good idea. You know, when your father bought the property, oil and gas prices were near an all-time low. The minerals wouldn't have added more value, so they probably weren't held out of the sale. But that land is at the edge of the Anadarko Basin. I bet not only the land has appreciated, but also the mineral rights."

The doorbell rang and as Will grabbed his wallet to pay the pizza delivery man he said, "We should look at the paperwork to see if the purchase includes the underground mineral rights. It also makes me wonder if Mom owns the mineral rights to her property."

PART II

Deep Drilling Boom

Chapter 17

The oil and gas exploration business in Oklahoma was slow for the next several years. Low wellhead prices slowed new exploration, forcing the import of more crude oil from the Middle East, which soon supplied over half of the US demand. Major oil companies and small independent producers alike struggled to make a profit. By 1973 import quotas and declining production created a shortage of both furnace oil and gasoline.

In October 1978, Congress deregulated the price of natural gas sold intrastate and natural gas produced from below 15,000 feet. This provided a new incentive for Oklahoma drillers to search for huge reservoirs of natural gas believed to be deep in Oklahoma's Anadarko Basin, and attracted money from local investors, local and national banks, and Wall Street.

1978

It was a crisp fall morning at McCall's Production Equipment Company before the office opened, a favorite productive time for Will. He'd been in the office for over an hour, catching up on administrative chores, scheduling new orders and new projects, and approving checks issued for supplier invoices—administrative tasks more easily completed without interruption from the phone, the shop, or family.

He slumped in his chair as he eyed the stack of recently received invoices, many overdue for payment. The McCall products made from these materials had shipped, but the customers hadn't paid. A longer manufacturing cycle from order entry to shipment caused a cash flow problem for most small manufacturing businesses. The good news was a healthy backlog of orders.

Roberta Flack's smooth voice floated from a radio on his credenza singing "Killing Me Softly."

He identified with the lyrics. Their cash flow problem was killing McCall's Production Equipment Company softly, too.

The back door banged as someone came in, snapping him from his troubling thought, and a moment later a soft voice said, "Good morning, Will."

"Good morning, Betty. How are you today?"

"I'm good, thanks. You're in early. Trying to sort out the invoices we can pay?"

"Yes, as a matter of fact. How about our receivables; are we expecting some payments today?"

"I hope so, and I'll be making more collection calls again today."

Betty Jennings was a petite lady in her early forties, a former telephone operator with a trained, velvet-smooth voice. Johanna hired her when their previous receptionist returned to teaching. Betty's organizational skills and pleasing personality were unexpected bonuses. She quickly became adept at collecting overdue customer invoices.

Will was reviewing supplier folders containing printed checks for payment of old invoices when the office phone rang. His Timex watch read 7:15, about the normal time for the first ring of a Monday morning. He heard Betty pick it up and her usual pleasant tone answered, "McCall's Production Equipment... I will check and see. Who's calling, please?" Will watched her put the call on hold, turn, and walk a few steps to his office door.

"It's a George Martin asking for you. Shall I take a message?"

Will's face broke into a smile. "Really, George Martin? He's an old friend. I'll pick it up in here."

Betty closed the door on her way out as Will picked up his receiver and punched line 1. "Wow, the real George Martin returns! How are you and where are you?"

"I moved here recently from Tulsa. Working at Vinson Supply, and I know your company's a big customer. Have you got some time this morning? I was hoping we could mix a little business with some catching up."

"Sure. In fact, now's a good time, before it gets hectic around here."

"I'll be there in less than ten minutes," George answered.

Will hung up and walked to Betty's office to let her know his roommate from OU would be dropping by. "I heard he'd recently gone to work for Vinson Supply. Even though we're old friends, I expect he'll ask for payment on their overdue invoices. The Vinson file is on Mom's desk. Would you get it, and then let me know when he arrives? Thanks."

Vinson was an important supplier of the control valves and gas regulators used on McCall separators and storage tanks. They were also a distributer for several manufacturers, including US Steel, a major manufacturer of oil well casing.

Soon, Betty walked into Will's open office door, handed him the Vinson file, and said, "Mr. Martin is here. Can I show him back?"

Will said yes and opened the file. As expected, the invoices with checks for payment were there. He turned the radio off, then looked up to see the tall, sandy-haired man he'd known since high school approaching his door. He met George at the door with outstretched arms.

"Hey! George. It's really good to see you. It's been too long."

George met him with a strong bear hug, familiar to all who knew the man well. "Sorry to drop in on short notice."

Betty, standing behind him said, "Can I get you some coffee, Mr. Martin?"

"Yes, thank you, just black," he answered.

Will turned to grab his favorite coffee mug, which was scratched and chipped with faded lettering that read *Oilfield Trash and Proud of It*. He handed it to Betty. "Get me a refill too, please."

"Love your mug," George said. "I have a similar one. Before we get into business, let me say how sorry I am that I couldn't be at your dad's funeral. He was a good man and was respected by all who knew him or worked with him."

"Thanks, George. He left us too early, and we all miss him. Please, sit. Where have you been? What have you been up to?"

"After the summer we spent with Loffland in the oil patch, it took me two more years to finish school. I knew you'd dropped out to help with the family business. I bounced around in several jobs before starting with Vinson, working over in Tulsa. I bring good news and some not so good. Oh, but before I forget it, I saw pictures of your original buildings, and this new facility looks great."

"Thanks. Our sales growth forced the expansion of both shop and office space. We scrapped the old trailer house office a year ago. Now the workflow is much more efficient."

George said, "The good news is, the relief valves and pressures regulators you ordered some time ago will ship this week. On the other hand, I have to ask when we can expect payment on the February invoices."

Will leaned back in his chair and picked up the Vinson file. "Thanks, George. Getting those regulators is a tremendous help." Opening the file, he continued, "And I'm happy to give you checks to cover the overdue invoices." He handed two checks to George. "My apologies for the slow payment. We went through a dry spell, waiting on a big check from Kerr-McGee. We value our relationship and support from suppliers like Vinson."

George put the checks in his briefcase. "We appreciate your loyalty to us, as well."

"These new facilities have helped us in many ways, but the loan payments added to our existing cash flow problem. We're no longer just a salvage and rework shop. Now, half of our business is new, larger fabricated systems, customized and requiring more materials and controls with long lead times. Our payment terms are thirty days, but our average receivable takes about twice that to clear. The line of credit we established years ago isn't adequate for the longer manufacturing cycle. We need to find a larger line of credit, or some additional funding."

"All small businesses have that issue," George replied. "The major oil companies like to use us as a bank. Unfortunately, today's high interest rates encourage that behavior."

"Our new products business requires longer manufacturing cycle times. It's profitable as long as we can avoid going to the bank for short-term financing."

"Just hang in there. This industry is about to boom again. If the Fed will loosen the purse strings on the money supply, interest rates'll come down and loans could be justified on the return of capital. Business will also improve if the price of oil continues to climb past $40 a barrel."

Betty returned with their coffee. "Sorry it took so long. I had to make a fresh pot."

George sipped the coffee while Will said, "I hope you're right. The recent price deregulation of natural gas below 15,000 feet will be a huge stimulus to our industry. The futures price of intrastate gas has already risen to about $2 per thousand cubic feet, and I think Oklahoma independents, funded by hungry banks and new investors, will soon be drilling for the deep gas in the Anadarko Basin."

"I'm hearing the pipeline companies are starving for new gas and willing to sign take-or-pay contracts on the new gas, another market and price driver," George added. "That's another factor pushing up the wellhead price and encouraging investors and banks to finance those multi-million-dollar deep wells."

Will was familiar with the future potential. "Right. It'll be expensive and risky to reach that deep gas. I'll be interested to see where that kind of money comes from. Local banks don't have the capital reserves or loan limits to finance that kind of venture, and most independents don't have the proven reserves for the collateral required."

George added, "Today's independent operator has a good chance of reaching the deep gas, and producing it safely, thanks to new technology, tools, and materials available. But first we need the higher wellhead price this deregulation promises."

"I think you're right, George. The next several years could be great. I hope Vinson can continue to work with us until I find a solution to the cash flow problem."

George took another gulp of coffee and stood up. "I'd love to continue our talk, but I need to get going. I've got to leave town later today. Thanks for the checks. We need to find time to catch up on the last several years. How's your mother doing, and Stephanie? I heard she got married."

"Oh, they're both fine. Mom is still working on the financial side and is our HR person. Stephanie and her husband are running their own service company."

"Good for her," George replied. "I had quite a crush on her in high school and was sorry to hear she dropped out of college. Here's my card. Let's get together when I get back."

Will walked around his desk. "And here's mine. Lunch for sure. Give me a call. I felt bad about missing your wedding that summer after my junior year. When

Dad died, I committed to help Mom keep this business going. I'm sorry we lost touch during that time." He followed his friend to the front door.

George looked back with a furrowed brow. "It's partly my fault. I've been dealing with divorce problems most of this year. It was final a month ago. It's a long story. I'll explain later."

"Damn, George, I'm sorry. I didn't know."

"Which reminds me, how about you? Time for anyone else in your busy life?"

"Yes, I met someone not long after Dad's death. Another interesting story I'll share when we have time. Call me when you're back in town and I'll make the time."

With questions still hanging, they shook hands with a one-armed bear hug and exchanged goodbyes.

After George left, Will headed to his mother's office. "Mornin', Mom. We need to talk about our cash flow issues."

Before she could return the greeting, her desk phone rang. "Let me answer this call. It may be the bank."

Johanna answered, "McCall's Production Equipment....Well, hello, JD, I wasn't expecting to hear from you." After listening, she spoke again. "JD, I don't have time to discuss that right now. I'm waiting for a call from our bank. How 'bout I call you back tomorrow morning?" A pause. "Okay, talk to you then."

She hung up and looked up at Will. "He wanted to talk about our property, and whether we've ever leased it for drilling. Our acreage is on the far eastern end of the Anadarko Basin. Not prime oil and gas lease property. Besides, I'm not interested in selling the mineral rights."

"You're probably right. Your acreage would be

more valuable if they drill a successful well next door in Caddo County."

Johanna changed the subject. "Who was in your office so early? I came in to return a call to Steph. She's under a lot of stress, trying to raise two children and help run their service business. I know it's difficult to be a full-time mother and businesswoman, but I don't have any easy answers for her. Especially since I don't think Charley carries any of the administrative load. Maybe he can't."

"It was George Martin, of all people," Will replied. "We had a good but short visit because he's leaving town this afternoon. He's working for Vinson Pipe and Supply, whose invoices are late getting paid. Here's the file back. You had the checks in the file marked hold, but I gave them to him. I explained our cash flow problem, and he promised they'd hold them until the first of the month. We need to cover them and deal with our limited credit line." Frustration made his voice sharper than he intended.

His mother smiled. "I was going to mail those checks today. I put that big Kerr-McGee check in the night deposit late yesterday, so we should be covered." She reached for her pack of Marlboros and lit one up. "Sorry I missed George. Haven't seen him for years. How are he and Judy doing?"

"They've divorced."

"Oh, no. They were the poster couple for high school sweetheart marriages. What happened?"

"He didn't have time to explain. We agreed to get together when he's back in town next week. Now, you and I need to deal with this cash flow problem," he insisted. "We can only juggle accounts for so long before we lose customers. I always heard Dad say finding new customers is a lot harder, and more expensive, than keeping existing ones. I expect that also applies to suppliers who could cut us off or require upfront payment before shipping. We really need a long-term loan or a bigger revolving credit line."

Johanna exhaled after a long drag on her Marlboro, then leaned forward and said, "Neither a borrower nor lender be. That's what my Papa always said. He was a stubborn and proud man who lived by those words. He kept his butcher shop on a solid financial base without a bank loan, and I'm sure it limited the growth of his shop. He survived slow times because he didn't have loan payments to make. I think we've just got to manage the cash flow problem. We can increase quoted delivery lead times, and pursue more of the smaller, less complicated systems we can execute quickly and efficiently, to keep within our means. Quote a higher price and longer lead time on the big custom jobs."

Will listened patiently to the grandfather lesson, though their company had grown well past the one-man shop his father started and needed a financing solution commensurate with a larger, more complex business.

He replied, "Common sense agrees with your conservative philosophy, and for grandfather's small family butcher shop I'm sure it was best. But we're a growing business in a big, competitive industry that's moving into a period of expansion, maybe even a boom. We need the financial tools to maintain our current business, plus additional capital to take advantage of increases in demand. We may not have a choice, even though loan rates are out of sight. If this growing demand continues, we should be able to build higher loan costs into the product price."

Johanna stuffed out the Marlboro in her ashtray and leaned back in her chair with a strained expression. "Yes, you're probably right. My repeat of Papa's conservative philosophy is to remind us that, while we need this expanded line of credit, we should be careful not to get over-extended. We collateralized our current credit line against receivables, and I'm not sure what collateral we'll need for a larger, long-term revolving credit line. We may also need to look at private lending institutions instead of banks—except those guys will want an ownership percentage for a large cash infusion."

"George offered to come back to me with a name or two we could contact for additional funding. Shall I give you those contacts so you can make the inquiries? Or should I pursue them?"

"Let's do it together."

Chapter 18

After graduation, Phil Pederson started working at First City Bank of Oklahoma City, majority owned by the Pederson family for two generations. His father and uncle expected him to join the bank and follow their path to management. That sounded good to Phil—until he worked there for a year.

He found it boring, and his peers resented his family connections. Although he liked the bank environment and the banker image of well-tailored suit and tie that complimented his tall stature and natural good looks, Phil wanted a position that offered a broader range of experience.

Phil and Erin McCall Pederson lived in a middle-income suburb of Oklahoma City near his parents' home in upscale Nichols Hills. On their sixth wedding anniversary, they were driving home from dinner at the senior Pederson home when Erin broke a long silence.

"It was nice of your folks to have us over on our anniversary. I had a nice evening, only somewhat spoiled by the continuing questions of why we haven't given them grandchildren."

Her voice grew sharper as she went on. "Correction, why *I* haven't given them grandchildren. I've had it with the subtle, and sometimes not so subtle, criticism from your family. Enough of their second-guessing our efforts to start a family."

Phil didn't comment, so Erin continued. "You and I need to make some decisions and changes. I know you're frustrated, too, and more than a little bored at the bank. You have more potential and ambition than to sit under your father's thumb pushing paper on a clerk's salary, while I'm expected to keep up appearances at social events and bear grandchildren. We need to lead our own lives without their incessant advice, well-meaning as it might be."

"You're right. I'm not happy at the bank. It was a mistake to take the easy road and go to work there after college. No challenges, no real responsibility, even after my promotion to loan officer."

"We need to be able to make our own decisions without feeling the need to check with them about everything first."

Phil was quiet until he pulled into their driveway and turned off the car. "You're right, but what can we do about it? I don't want to put my résumé out on the street."

"Maybe we can make inquiries without broadcasting it," Erin answered. "I met a college friend for lunch last week, and she told me her uncle is the new CEO of a state bank on the northwest side of town. He's looking for an experienced loan officer. It's a commercial bank, but my friend says the owners want to expand into oil and gas loans. It might be your opportunity to break away from the family bank, take a different direction."

Erin got the number of Frank Wilson, her friend's uncle. Phil made the call, confident his years of bank loan experience would be enough to get the job. Sure enough, within two weeks, he was the new assistant VP of commercial loans at Oak Tree State Bank. He was out of his family's bank, with an opportunity to prove his worth on his own merit.

<><><>

Phil was busy in his new office that looked out on the banking floor. A popular Olivia Newton-John song was paying on a small radio on his credenza and Phil attempted to sing along to the new pop song.

"You better shape up, I need you man, my heart is set for you. You better shape up because there's nothing left for me to do. You're the one ..."

A knock sounded on his open door and Ms. Sunderland, Frank Wilson's secretary, entered with a big smile. "I love that song. It's from the movie *Grease*, right?"

He turned the radio off. "Good morning. Yes, a fun movie. Great tune! What's going on this morning?"

"Mr. Wilson would like to see you in his office." She raised eyebrows with a smile.

Phil started gathering the loan papers on his desk into a folder. "Tell him I'll be right there."

"Yes, come in," Frank replied to Phil's knock, then stood and shook his hand. "Good morning Phil." He walked around a large walnut desk. "Let's sit over here." They moved to a round table with four chairs.

Frank was in his early fifties, graying at the temples. His dark suit and power tie projected the successful banker, and Phil had heard the man had both a wealth of experience in the oil and gas industry and valuable contacts in the financial world, from state regulators to wealthy investors.

"I had hoped we could talk sooner, but it's been a busy time for me," Frank said. "Plus, I thought you could use the time to get settled in a new environment. I'm guessing it's a tremendous change, moving from a large bank your family built to this smaller state bank."

Phil expected the question. "The change is a welcome one for me. I view this as an opportunity to make a difference rather than just follow in my father's footsteps."

"Good," Frank replied. "And let me say, I'm happy to have you on my team. Besides your experience as a loan officer, you have business and community ties that could be beneficial as this bank pursues a much different loan market."

Frank leaned back comfortably. "Oak Tree State Bank was chartered as a state bank with a strong balance sheet, but failed to find enough commercial loans to reach the revenue and profit goals set by the owners.

"This last recession dried up traditional commercial markets for state banks like us. High interest rates have made loans too expensive for small businesses, and the large corporations are issuing bonds rather than borrowing from a bank. I was hired to make the bank profitable, and I'm going to do that by moving into a new area. Are you familiar with Penn Square Bank's recent move into oil and gas loans?"

"Somewhat," Phil said. "I know they're making some big loans, so big it seems they'd be beyond Penn's loan limits and out of their league. But I don't have any firsthand knowledge of it."

"What they're writing are large natural gas exploration loans. That's where I want this bank to go as well. We need to find a different market to grow our bank, and I think Penn Square has found that new lucrative market in the oil and gas exploration business. I want to start an oil and gas loan department, and I want you to help me do that."

"Great, count me in," Phil answered eagerly. "I've read about Robert Hefner's exploration work to find the deep natural gas in the Anadarko Basin. He drilled a 24,000-foot gas well, the deepest one ever, ten years ago and the well flow tested close to twenty million cubic feet per day. It turned out to be a commercial failure because the price of natural gas was at an all-time low, but he proved there's a lot of natural gas down there."

"That's right," Frank agreed. "Today the deregulation of natural gas produced from 15,000 feet is starting to drive up the price, forecasting wells like Hefner's could be profitable at some point. I just learned Mobil Oil has signed a contract with Hefner's company, GHK, to finance the drilling of one hundred leases in the Anadarko Basin, a deal potentially worth $200 million. That contract could be the start of the next energy boom. The increasing demand will continue to drive up the price of deep natural gas."

Frank leaned toward Phil. "Our opportunity is in the high-dollar loans that will be needed to drill a well to depths of 15,000 to 20,000 feet. As Hefner learned, it's high risk, technically difficult, and very expensive. But, if there is a huge natural gas reservoir down there, the return could be several times the cost."

"Agree," Phil said. "Family and friends tell me there are new high-strength alloy pipe and stronger joint designs that'll make the new deep wells more expensive but safer to drill. Again, promising big returns on the initial expense."

"Right. I'm glad you understand the business and what it takes. Penn Square has made big loans to Lammerts Oil and Longhorn Oil and Gas for deep well projects. Like us, they don't have the capital or loan limits to lend the millions necessary for these projects."

Phil opened his mouth but Frank asked the question for him. "So how are they doing it? They've been able to get larger upstream banks to participate in these loans, and Penn Square takes loan service and origination fees."

Frank slapped his knee. "That's exactly what we're going to do. If you and I can develop the tools and the upstream banks will participate...The potential return is huge, and these large national banks are eager to fund the multi-million-dollar ventures."

Phil listened intently, then questioned his boss. "I understand, but how do we make money selling these loans for a service and origination fee of, what, 1–3 percent? I know we need them since they have the large capital reserves and loan limits to take the enormous risks, but aren't we giving away the big money to the upstream bank, at current rates approaching 10 percent? Where's the money in it for us?"

"We hold back 1–2 percent, then charge a one percent origination fee, netting a 100 percent return immediately. Just a few of these multi-million-dollar loans could return many times more than we make on small business commercial loans. We write the loan, documenting the business opportunity, client's assets, and in-ground reserves, and collateralize it enough to convince the larger bank to fund it."

"I think I know where you're going," Phil interrupted. "Our loan servicing opens opportunities for additional personal loans, supplier loans, and loans to investors. It becomes the growth engine generating income from investor loans and account services."

"You got it," Frank said. "A new loan customer, say a lawyer, doctor, or business executive, may want to borrow against their assets to buy into these projects. Out-of-state money could flow into the bank—personal loans, commercial loans, real estate loans. We attract individual investors who can realize immediate tax write off for drilling costs."

Phil leaned forward, eyes opened wide, as his new boss drew him a picture of making big money in deep gas exploration loans. "It sounds like a brilliant plan. Where do we start? My family and I have friends that could be interested in these ventures. Maybe we can put together a reception to promote the risk/reward benefits of these exploration ventures."

"We have some upstream contacts to make and a new loan system to put in place first. I'll contact the same bank Penn Square is working with, Continental Illinois Trust of Chicago. Hopefully, they'll participate in similar loans we sign. Meanwhile, I want you to pull together the documentation, including the legal requirements, to put these deals on paper. I'm told Republic Bank in Dallas and Fidelity Bank here in town have the forms and know how to collateralize these oil and gas loans. Use your contacts to gather the documentation we need and get back to me. We'll also need to draft a business plan for board approval."

"I'm sure my father has contacts at Republic," Phil offered. "They can probably send me the documents for collateralizing in-ground oil reserves, and oil and gas loan forms. I also know a few individuals who invest in this risky, high-return type of investment. When we're ready, maybe invite investors and independent companies to a seminar on oil and gas investing."

"Yes, excellent," Frank said. "When we've got the loan tools and one or two large banks ready to participate, we can be more aggressive finding independents who have assets, experience, and need the millions necessary to start drilling."

Phil stood and extended his hand across the desk. "Thank you for the opportunity to work with you on this, Mr. Wilson. I'm excited about the potential."

Frank shook his hand with the words, "Good. If the bank is successful, you and I can benefit too."

Getting away from Dad's bank was the best move I ever made, Phil thought as he returned to his own office. *I'm going to make it big on my own.*

Chapter 19

1979

On the other side of town, increased production and the increase in the price of oil meant new income growth for C&S Trucking. Their strategy of capturing oil entrained in wastewater was paying off, doubling their income from trucking services. Charley and Stephanie bought a new, larger home to fit their growing family.

C&S Trucking was now selling pipe and services to Arnold Oil and Gas, funding the expansion of their yard and inventory of drill pipe, fittings and rig supplies. The expanded trucking yard, now a rectangular two-acre property, included a new office building and a vehicle maintenance bay.

Meanwhile, JD's Arnold Oil and Gas Company was growing because of incredible luck in corner drilling. This exploration strategy aims at tapping into the edge of a large producing reservoir by drilling within the well distance regulations near the calculated perimeter of a proven reservoir of oil, gambling to tap into a big reservoir through an extension, or corner, of the known reservoir. It's a low probability venture and production life is short; but if successful, the operator can use a percentage of the large reservoir as in-ground assets, collateral for borrowing exploration funds.

JD built a new four-thousand-square-foot ranch-style home with a swimming pool and a four-car garage with room for both a four-wheel-drive pickup with dual wheels and his new Chevy Suburban complete with cellular telephone. His new gold neck chain and custom cowboy boots with *JD* tooled in the leather fueled a new level of confidence and a new line of bullshit. He believed he could compete with the big boys for deep gas in the Anadarko Basin.

All he needed was money. A lot of money. At bourbon-and-Coke lunches with independent colleagues at Junior's, the favorite watering hole of Oklahoma City oilmen, JD learned about a new financing tool called a drilling fund, comprised of money from banks and individual investors in return for a share of the profits. At one of those lunches JD asked his attorney Mike Shalling to find out the legal and procedural steps necessary to start a drilling fund for Arnold Oil and Gas.

In his office on a frosty February morning in 1979, he got a call from the lawyer.

"Hey Mike, I hope you're calling about drilling funds."

"I am. I've been in touch with some people who can help you get started."

"Great. What do we do?"

"I've talked with a law firm that's written a few of these drilling fund programs, and they recommended we talk with Phil Pederson at Oak Tree State Bank. He can help you find the money to fund one or two drilling programs of this type. I called him and suggested we meet tomorrow at Cattleman's Steakhouse. We set it up for 7 p.m. Will that fit your schedule? Maybe we can work a deal over drinks."

"You betcha. I'll be there. I know Phil and Oak Tree, a small commercial bank. Do you think a state bank can fund a major drilling program? We're talking millions. I didn't think that bank would have the resources."

"They plan to partner with a large national bank who can write the big loans, up to five or ten million. I've heard Penn Square Bank has been doing the same thing with a Chicago bank. Additionally, there are brokerage houses and well-heeled individual investors hungry for the big money this deep natural gas can deliver."

"Mike, let's you and I meet there at 6:30. I need you to tell me more about how this works before the bankers arrive."

"Sounds good. See you then."

<><><>

JD brought Charley with him. They found Mike at the bar.

"What do ya say, Mike?" JD approached with an extended hand. "Thanks for setting this up. This is my son Charley. He runs a supply and service company we use. I brought him along for backup. In case we need some muscle. Ha, ha!"

The attempt at humor solicited a small grin from the attorney. "Okay, let's find a quiet table so we can talk."

The group moved to a table in the corner and Mike ordered a round of drinks, including a couple of Wild Turkey bourbons on the rocks for the Arnolds.

JD said, "Thanks." He was never one to fight over a bar tab.

"So, I'll lay out the typical framework for how a drilling fund is structured," Mike began. "Then when we get with the Jordan Smithson people, they'll elaborate, and you can ask your questions." He then explained how the fund works, with a pro forma legal description offered to banks and other prospective investors, with risk assessment, including historic returns on investments, complete with disclaimer of guarantees.

The three received their drinks and JD changed the subject to Oklahoma football. Let the lawyers and bankers worry about details and legal terms—that's what they were there for. The talk shifted to the next Texas-Oklahoma football game.

Mike interrupted JD to say, "They're here now. I see the hostess taking them to a back room. Let's take our drinks and follow them."

In the private dining room JD recognized Phil and three others about to be seated. Phil walked toward them but Mike spoke first.

"I'm Mike Shalling, and I think you know these gentlemen."

"Yes." Phil offered his hand. "JD, Charley. This is Dan Jordan and Bill Jennings, attorneys, and our bank president, Frank Wilson. Please join us." Eyeing their cocktails in hand, he added, "I see you've started without us."

"JD offered to buy me a drink, an offer I couldn't pass up. But it hasn't happened yet," Mike joked, and everyone chuckled, including JD, who took the bait.

"Sometimes I just forget and leave my wallet in

the truck." The reply gained understanding nods and awkward smiles.

Mike and the Arnolds took seats opposite the Oak Tree Bank party. Phil's group ordered cocktails and another round for JD and Charley. Hors d'oeuvres of calamari and peeled shrimp with a spicy cocktail sauce were served in the center of the table.

Phil opened the meeting by describing a typical drilling program. Then Dan Jordan explained the legal requirements and limits of both investors and operators.

Frank Wilson followed the legalese. "A couple of important points need to be made as potential operators or general partners. First, there should be a description of the leases and drilling schedules, so the investors and bankers can assess the risk for themselves. Second, a detail of current in-ground oil reserves, plus your company history of successful well production, and résumé of success finding oil and/or natural gas."

Typical of a true Okie oilman, JD was quick to respond with an embellished history of his company. He concluded with a question. "For a small state bank, Mr. Wilson, aren't you getting in a little over your head?"

"We know these deep gas wells are multi-million-dollar projects," Frank said. "Drilling them has an increasing cost structure. The first five thousand feet might cost up to $100,000 and take four to six weeks. To go from 5,000 feet to 15,000 feet can cost millions more and take six to nine months to complete."

Phil interjected, "As I'm sure you know, the payoff can be huge. A deep well could produce 10–20 million cubic feet a day of natural gas. With wellhead gas prices expected to reach five to seven dollars per thousand cubic feet, the well could pay off its cost within a month and then continue producing for years at full profit."

"We can manage these large loans just as Penn Square Bank has done," Frank said, "by gaining participation from larger national banks such as Continental Illinois Trust of Chicago and others who can provide the millions necessary to drill these deep wells. We'll take an origination fee and service fee, offering the balance to the big banks. They like this structure because they leave the servicing and collateralizing to us. We work with you to document assets and collateral— which is usually in-ground reserves."

"So, the drilling fund uses bank loans at astronomical rates?" JD asked.

"It's true the bank rates are high, but that's the source of the big money you need to reach the big natural gas," Phil said. "And if you strike the big gas, the pay back is several times the drilling costs. We can negotiate the interest rate down to a couple of points above prime. Plus, we can get some funding from individuals or private groups; that would lower the interest rate on the fund total."

"There ain't a lot of people that wealthy who want to put all their cash into drilling," Charley said. "How do we get them to buy in to our deal?"

"They don't have to put up as much cash as you think," Frank said. "Individual investors can now use a new loan instrument the banks are offering called a standby letter of credit. It's a statement from their bank of their deposited assets, such as CDs and savings. Individual investors subscribe to the drilling fund by putting up 10–25 percent of the assets in cash, and using a standby letter of credit for the rest. The general partner gets the cash and uses the letter of credit as collateral for the fund's bank loan."

Phil added, "Plus, tax laws now allow the investor to deduct the full letter of credit from his taxes, since the funds are part of the exploration costs, designated by the IRS as an at-risk investment. That law has stimulated considerable interest from not only individuals, but brokerage houses and Wall Street. Mark my words, this new instrument will attract a wide range of investors. Business executives, doctors, lawyers—anyone with significant assets."

"You'll get cash up front as the subscription money comes in," Frank said. "Long before you incur any drilling costs. The key is the tax advantage to the investor."

JD and Charley beamed at hearing how easy it might be to fund their dream projects going for deep gas. "Well boys, we just need to round up some investors." JD said.

Phil answered. "Yes, and this meeting might generate enough interest to take that next step. I'll reserve a private room at the Petroleum Club, and we'll host fifty people for a sit-down steak dinner, sometime around the first of the month. That gives us three weeks to get out invitations to anyone you know with a fat bank account who's ready to make big gas money. We can mail invitations as soon as we can put together a list of prospects. Mike will have a pro forma drilling fund ready to go for those in attendance, so they can take the paperwork with them."

"Or sign on the spot," JD said.

Phil continued, "We propose the fund be named Arnold Oil and Gas Drilling Fund 1. From the general response we've seen to this type of deal, plus the interest we expect from the promotional dinner and preliminary subscriptions, we project the total amount of the fund to be close to six million. That's our target. The final amount will depend on the individual interest. Then we offer the package to the Chicago banks for additional funding to reach the target, or even acquire more. I'll get back to everyone when Mike has the pro forma drafted. In the meantime, we'll plan the promotional dinner and contact Chicago banks to determine what their participation could be. Questions?"

JD shook his head. "Nope. Let's get another round of drinks and some menus. All this talk of drilling for big gas money is making me hungry."

<><><>

Stephanie had just turned on the ten o'clock news when Charley arrived home, a little tipsy. He dropped his keys on the tray near the front door.

"Come in here and tell me about the dinner with JD and bankers."

Charley leaned against the door jamb. "It was fun. Exciting news. If the drilling fund works like they say, we could make a ton of money. Oak Tree Bank and some legal guys are going to put together a fund and raise money for Dad's company to drill for deep Anadarko natural gas. Investors and big banks are willing to put up millions of dollars at high interest rates. We're talking millions to drill the wells, and *hundreds* of millions in return. We—you and me—could invest as a limited partner with our own money and get a big tax deduction for drilling costs."

"We can't afford that."

"Yeah, we can, 'cause we don't have to have the

money. They let you use what's called a letter of credit from the bank. It says we're worth it, so we may not have to give 'em any cash."

"It sounds like this is all about JD and Arnold Oil and Gas. What's in it for C&S?"

Charley paused, seeming to struggle for an answer. Then he said, "Well, I suppose so. The fund will be organized under Arnold Oil and Gas, with their name, and it'll be the general partner and operator. But we could be their major supplier for all the piping materials, tools, and other materials."

"Hmm. Maybe you're right," Stephanie acknowledged. Charley may have stumbled into a good deal again. "I can see how we could make a lot of money being the major supplier to Arnold Oil and Gas—whether they strike the big gas or not. But we'd need to have a stronger connection with the company. We should meet with your dad and try to get a contract. Or at least his word that he'll purchase the specialty tools and the drill pipe and well casing from C&S."

"Do you know George Martin, an old friend of Will's?"

"Yeah, I remember George."

"He's a sales engineer for Vinson Supply. He sells regulators and control valves to Will. His company is also a distributor for US Steel casing and tubing, and they're now supplying high-strength alloy casing with special joints that can withstand the conditions drillers are facing in these deeper Anadarko wells. We need to contact him and find out what materials are used in the deep wells. Maybe we can get a stocking discount, or a stocking fee for holding his casing for immediate delivery."

Chapter 20

Stephanie called JD at 8 a.m. on the dot the next morning with a business plan in mind.

"Charley gave me some feedback on your dinner meeting last night. This drilling fund plan sounds promising for Arnold Oil and Gas. We need to talk about how C&S Trucking can be part of these deep projects."

"Now, you know I'll always look out for my son and your company. What's on your mind?"

Stephanie wasn't ready to discuss details; she needed time to research the needs C&S could fill for Arnold O&G, and the business structure that would tie both companies closer. This call was to get a jump on the situation.

"I'm trying to detail out something I think you'll be interested in," she said. "Can we get together later this week for lunch, maybe Wednesday or Thursday?"

"All right. How about I pick you up and we'll go over to Junior's for lunch, say 11:30 on Wednesday?"

"Perfect."

Knowing JD, Stephanie began to prepare for what would likely be a male-dominated, don't-worry-your-pretty-little-head-about-it-you-wouldn't-understand, conversation. Rather than being defensive, she wanted a firm business plan that had profit potential and legal credibility. She picked up the phone to call Sam Buchanan.

<><><>

JD pulled into Junior's with Stephanie just before noon. As much as the food, he liked the atmosphere, and being seen here. The oil industry's best and worst gathered at the place for business lunches that included million-dollar deals scratched on a paper napkin, sketchy documentation of handshake agreements made over hardballs or a pitcher of draft beer.

The hostess seated them at a window booth and they ordered drinks, his usual gin and tonic and iced tea for Stephanie.

"All right, here's the deal," she said. "I'd like C&S Trucking and Arnold Oil and Gas to form a holding company together. Maybe call it Sooner Development or Sooner Oil and Gas. By combining the businesses into a holding company, we can leverage the total assets for loans as well as reduce costs. Sooner becomes the entity that contracts for drilling ventures, and buys the pipe, drilling mud, and other tools through C&S at retail, or even inflated prices, and charges the costs to the well. Arnold Oil and Gas would be the operator for Sooner at whatever price the market will bear."

"Who would own this holding company?"

"Both of us," Stephanie said. "The bank or attorney that prepares the paperwork to organize the holding company can issue shares in proportion to the assets of each company. They complete whatever paperwork's required. The attorney I consulted suggests it be limited liability partnership. That'll shield our personal assets from liability claims or lawsuits against the holding company. Let's sit down with a third-party adviser and work out the deal, so it's a win-win for both of us. If at any point during the process you decide you're unhappy with any of it, you can call it off."

<><><>

A week later Stephanie met JD and his attorney Mike Shalling at the offices of Smith Barney. C&S Trucking had an account there and knew the firm had the knowledge to set up the new holding company. Both companies were listed as equal partners in Sooner Oil and Gas, LLC. Documents outlined the assets and liabilities of both companies, and stipulated that all decisions, including those on financial ventures, loans, and investments, must be approved by both parties.

Leaving the Smith Barney offices, Stephanie turned to her father-in-law. "I need to get back, but we need to talk more about the details. How about I get Charley and meet you at Cattleman's around 7 p.m.?"

"Sounds good. I've got some questions and concerns as well. Plus, we need to get moving on the drilling fund we talked about a couple of weeks ago. We'll see you over there."

Stephanie stopped walking. "Did you say *we*? Are you bringing someone from the company?"

"Nope. I've been dating a lady I've known for many years. Her name's Julie. She's an executive secretary at Kerr-McGee and knows all about oil and gas leases. I think you and Charley will like her. See you then." He walked away.

Chapter 21

The following Sunday, a cool but sunny October afternoon, Will and Christi turned off the blacktop highway onto the gravel road that led to Johanna's house. Johanna planned a family picnic, and all the McCalls were invited.

Will found a parking space on the circular drive next to a variety of unfamiliar cars. "That must be the Arnold's new Chevy Suburban, and I don't recognize the BMW. I'm guessing it's Erin and Phil's. They're all about keeping up with the Country Club set. I know the oil business has improved, but I doubt the banking business will make you rich overnight. Maybe he just spent his bonus from last year."

"Now, Will. It's a family gathering. Let's try to keep it positive. I made some queso dip and brought a couple big bags of Fritos. The beer and dip are in that small cooler. If you'll carry it, I've got the Fritos."

They rounded the garage and stepped onto the patio as Johanna handed Phil a tray of hamburger patties for the grill. She turned and greeted them with open arms. "Hi, kids. It's so good to see you. It's been weeks and I'm eager to hear what all you've been up to."

Christi pulled the dip out of the cooler. "We brought queso and Fritos. Where should I put them?"

"Just set 'em in the middle of the picnic table. Everyone can help themselves."

Johanna followed Christi to the table and picked up her cigarette from an ashtray nearby.

Will set the cooler down and walked to Erin, who was sitting in the shade near the house. "Is that your BMW out front?"

"Yes, but it's not new. Phil's grandfather made us a deal we couldn't refuse. They sold two of their cars since his grandmother doesn't drive anymore. We love it. There's plenty of room and it's a high-performance sedan. Phil says it takes the road curves like it's on rails."

Stephanie stepped out from the kitchen. "Hi, bro. How's business?"

"Good, and improving for a change. We're not getting rich yet, but we're covering increased costs and paying down a couple of old loans. How 'bout you and Charley? Is the run up in oil prices translating into new service business?"

"Yeah. In fact, we're expecting new well prospects so we're going to expand our supply inventory and the yard. You know we merged with Arnold O&G, didn't you? We set up a holding company called Sooner Oil and Gas, LLC. It's already proven to be a smart move. We'll gain considerable business from Arnold O&G without competition, and we can pass the increased cost on to the investors. Very profitable for both companies."

"If I understand the business model, Arnold, under the joint venture of Sooner, purchases most of their tool and pipe needs for projects named in the drilling fund through C&S. Right? Is that legal?"

"Of course it is! We had attorneys set it all up, and all costs are listed for the limited partners in a statement. If you're implying JD should shop around for the low-cost supplier, I can assure you the fund partners are more interested in getting the well drilled and producing ASAP, because the return far outweighs any difference in the cost."

"How many deep wells are planned?" Will asked.

"JD doesn't talk to me about those details, but I know he's purchased at least a half dozen leases in Caddo and has talked to Mom about drilling in Grady County. He's also discussed joint venture deals in Beckham and Roger Mills Counties."

Charley walked up as she added, "You may have heard GHK has been working on a $30 million deal with Mobil Oil to drill several deep wells in the Elk City area."

"Will, you need to invest in a drilling fund or a working interest," Charley said. "This is a natural gas production boom that could dwarf the oil booms of the past. Bigger gas money than ever from deep natural gas reservoirs. This is the opportunity of a lifetime."

"It's also an enormous risk," Will answered. "There aren't many successful twenty-thousand-foot gas wells."

"Hefner produced from a deep well back in the late sixties," Charley reminded him. "He demonstrated a production potential of one hundred million cubic feet a day. At the current price of $7 per thousand cubic feet, that's $700,000 per day. Twenty million a month! So what if it costs five or six million to drill it? You get the full return of that investment in about a week. If the pundits are right and this boom only lasts a couple of years, investors will still make hundreds of millions. Some analysts are predicting the price of gas could reach $10 in the next 12–18 months."

"Now you know why I wanted out of the family salvage business," Stephanie added. "You work your ass off for peanuts, with lots of bills, not to mention the headaches of managing a grind-it-out business. No thanks. A couple of these gas wells and we'll retire to a beach and spend our weekends flying to Las Vegas."

"It's tempting, I agree. But Christi and I have all we can manage right now. We've got a mortgage on the house, and the company is stretching its credit line. Luckily, business is growing, and I expect it to do better if the boom continues as you predict."

Johanna joined the group, exhaling a cloud of Marlboro smoke. "What are you all talking about?"

"Mom, I thought you were off the cigarettes," Will said. "You told me at the office you quit, and I believed you. In fact, I haven't seen you smoke there since."

"Yes. I have quit—at the office. But at times like this, when I'm having a beer and relaxing my family, I enjoy smoking a cigarette."

Stephanie answered her mother's question. "We've been discussing the growing boom in drilling for the deep Anadarko Basin natural gas. You should invest in one of JD's drilling funds. It'd pay off big and you could retire."

"Steph, you know I'm not a gambler. Your brother and I worked long and hard to grow the business and I have no wish to gamble it away."

"You gotta take a big risk to get a big payoff," Charley commented.

"Yes; but historically, most people looking for black gold went broke. This deep gas is just another invisible treasure at the end of the rainbow. There'll be a few who make money, but most will go bankrupt."

Their conversation ended when Erin announced from the table, "Hey everybody, Phil says the hamburgers are about done. Wash your hands and get your drink. We'll sit down at the table in about five minutes."

Chapter 22

The following Tuesday, Phil and Frank took an early AA flight to Chicago for a mid-morning arrival. They were going to a meeting with two officers of Continental Illinois Trust, Don Williams, Vice President of Oil and Gas Loans, and Senior Vice President John Littleton. They hoped to gain participation in some large exploration loans to Sooner Oil and Gas, LLC and two other independents, backed up by company profiles, drilling fund commitments, and in-ground reserves.

Walking off the plane at O'Hare Airport, Frank said, "Let's find a phone. I requested a lunch meeting. Don's secretary said they were available but to call her when we arrive to confirm the time and place."

"That would be great," Phil said. "The more time we can get with them, the better. Time to get to know them. As you know, business deals are easier made with friends. Plus, we can use the time to get a better understanding of their requirements to participate in these oil and gas loans. We need to wrap it up by two to get back here for our return flight at 4:30."

They stopped at a bank of pay phones in the airport gate area and Frank reached Don Williams's secretary, explained they had arrived, and asked if a lunch meeting was still possible. After a moment he nodded and said, "Okay, we should be there in about 30 minutes." He hung up. It was 10:45.

"Don will have lunch with us, but John Littleton has a previous engagement. She said to call from the main lobby receptionist's desk when we get to the bank."

An airport cab let them out at the Continental headquarters on LaSalle Street in Chicago's financial district. The two native Okies were in awe of the Corinthian columns on the front of a massive stone building like the Federal Reserve Bank. Their wonderment continued onto the huge marble banking floor, all part of an image of strength and wealth. In the large lobby, a customer service desk sat in their path. Phil stepped up, gave the receptionist their names, and explained their appointment with Don Williams.

In less than ten minutes, Don arrived, strolling across the expansive floor. Dressed in a dark suit, white shirt, and tight-patterned red tie, he presented the banker image: a tall, thin, well-groomed, mid-forties Midwesterner who, they later learned, grew up in Kansas.

"Gentlemen, welcome to Chicago, and Continental Illinois."

After introductions, he said, "It's a lovely day, so I thought we could walk a couple of blocks. My secretary reserved a table for us at The Berghoff, a Chicago fixture for many years. You can leave your briefcases here at the desk; they'll be safe until we return."

During the ten-minute walk, the men exchanged personal histories, experience, and the usual who-knew-who. For his age, Don had held a wide range of jobs in the oil industry, including several international assignments, before joining Continental.

Once seated near a window of the established German restaurant, they ordered a draft beer Don recommended.

"As I expect you know, Continental has taken participation in Penn Square loans involving drilling projects in Oklahoma," Don said. "I understand from our phone discussion you have a couple of similar oil and gas loan opportunities. I'm sure you've realized the commercial loan market is dying. Also, new banking laws limit us from adding satellite banks. Securities brokers and other financial companies are picking up small retail loans, personal loans, and savings accounts. Large corporations can issue bonds, convertible stocks, and other paper to raise capital, thus avoiding today's high interest rates."

The waiter returned for their orders. Don recommended the luncheon steak. "This restaurant prides itself in offering corn-fed beef from Illinois. It's hard to beat. I know that might sound out of place to Oklahomans who raise Angus cattle, but trust me, you'll be impressed."

After everyone ordered a steak, Don went back to his comments on the status of business at large banks.

"As I was saying, large national banks like ours need to find new loan markets. The increased interest in exploring for deep natural gas looks to satisfy that need, and Continental has a long, conservative history of successful loans in the oil and gas market. We're now taking on more risk with these exploration loans, believing it necessary to grow. And many Oklahoma oil and gas independents have convinced us there's a huge quantity of natural gas in the deep reservoirs in Oklahoma. To balance the risk, we've increased our reserves, and our shareholder's return for the first half of this year was an unprecedented 15 percent. We're the leader in banking today, as evidenced by the recent election of our president to the American Bankers Association."

"Outstanding," Frank said. "We're excited to offer you additional loan opportunities that will benefit both of us. When we get back to your office, Phil will present the details of our prospects."

The three finished their luncheon steaks, Frank paid the bill, and they returned to the bank's fifteenth floor. Don's secretary escorted Frank and Phil to a large conference room while Don excused himself to check on his boss, John Littleton.

Within minutes, a middle-aged gentleman dressed in the banker uniform of the dark suit with a colorful pocket handkerchief and striped tie led Don into the room and offered his hand in greeting.

"Good afternoon, gentlemen. I'm John Littleton. Welcome, and thank you for visiting Continental."

Don introduced the Oak Tree visitors from Oklahoma.

Shaking Mr. Littleton's hand, Frank said, "When we arrived this morning, we thought we had arrived at the Federal Reserve. Your bank building is magnificent, and projects the financial strength I'm sure you're proud of. I'm sorry you weren't able to join us for the wonderful lunch at The Berghoff."

"We look forward to seeing you back again, and I'll have another chance to join you." Mr. Littleton said. "I understand you have some clients wanting to make exploration loans. I'm confident we have the capital that can help them."

"Yes," Frank answered. "We're here today to show you some oil and gas loan opportunities, hoping Continental can participate with us in making exploration loans to independent oil and gas companies in our state. We understand you've given substantial support, in loan participation, to our neighbor Penn Square Bank and Trust, and I think you'll find these are similar opportunities. These exploration companies are experienced operators capable of tapping into the deep natural gas deposits in western Oklahoma. I'd like Phil to outline these companies, their histories, existing reserves, and capabilities to be successful in these rather expensive ventures."

Phil's presentation covered loans signed by Oak Tree for Sooner Oil and Gas Drilling Fund and a summary of the prospectus with a target amount of five million dollars. He explained Oak Tree's desire to recover fees for originating and servicing the accounts. He also offered similar loan participations for two other independents, each requesting amounts under $5 million.

"As I'm sure you know," he concluded, "our loan limitations prevent us from taking on these multi-million-dollar prospects without participation from you or another national bank that has the reserves to back these large loans. Continental is the first large bank we've offered these loan participations. Are you comfortable with the amounts and fees as described? Do you have questions?"

"I think this is a good start," John answered. "The amounts themselves are not a problem and your fees are within what we've paid for similar participation. We'll need to have our people and engineering consultants review the data you've given us. Assuming it's all in line with our usual requirements, I'm confident we can move forward to participate at some level. We'll want a breakdown on where the loan money will be spent and to confirm the value of their reserves in support. The loan total is in line with others we've written in the industry. We'll establish the final loan amounts from our evaluation, and they may want some additional background details. I assume you're leaving this documentation with us?"

Phil said, "Yes, of course," and pushed the documents over to him. "Included is the information I presented our standard loan forms for each borrower with final amounts left open."

"Great. We should be able to complete our review in a few days—before you need to look for additional loan sources," Don concluded with a smile.

Frank and Phil beamed in the positive response from the Chicago bankers and commented on the way to the airport how Continental was eager to beat cross-town rival, First National Bank of Chicago, to this loan market. It was another sign that large financial institutions were eager to get a share of the potential return on the coming boom in natural gas discoveries.

Frank and Phil returned home that afternoon, confident of some loan support from Continental. How much support was unknown. They had stretched the estimate of the reserves to justify the requested loan amounts, so a reservoir engineering company might challenge the estimate. That could reduce the amount of the loan, though it rarely caused an outright rejection.

Phil called JD Arnold the next day. "We met with the Continental Illinois Trust loan officers yesterday. The meeting went well. Their response was encouraging. They'll review our loan request and the background documents detailing the assets of Sooner Oil and Gas, years of experience, and the drilling schedule. I expect we'll hear from them within the next week to ten days."

"You mean they listened to your sales pitch and didn't go for it?"

"No, not at all. They asked for time to evaluate the estimated reserves we reported and other data presented. As you know, most independents like yourself have few hard assets to collateralize a loan, so most lenders look for proven in-ground reserves. The value of those reserves can be debatable among reservoir engineers. The risk lies with our estimate versus a third-party engineering review. If they determine we overestimated reserves, the approved loan amount will be less. But I happen to know that Penn Square Bank has received large loan participation from Continental for GHK and others with similar or less documentation."

"So you think it'll happen?"

"Yes," Phil confirmed. "I'm confident we'll get some loan backing. How much they'll offer is the question. Can you tell me the percentage or number of individual investors subscribed?"

"I believe the fund is short of a full subscription by about $3 million."

"That sounds about right. We requested more than that from Continental, so even if they don't give us as much as we asked for, we should make the fund's goal. I'll call you when I hear from them."

The next day's *Wall Street Journal*'s Markets listed

the 30-day futures of natural gas at seven dollars per one thousand cubic feet. On Monday, Phil received a call from Don Williams, saying that the requested loans were approved by their loan committee and that documentation confirming the loan was in the mail.

Two days later, Ms. Sunderland entered Phil's office and said, "Mr. Wilson said this envelope should have gone to you." She handed him a large manila mailing envelope with the return address and logo of Continental Illinois Trust.

"Great. We've been expecting this." Enclosed were a letter signed by John Littleton and loan documents for participating in loans to Sooner Oil and Gas and two others. They approved a loan of $3.55 million to Sooner Oil and Gas Company, and smaller participations for the others.

Phil gathered the documents and rushed to Frank's office.

Tapping on his open door, Phil exclaimed, "We got Continental's letter of participation for $9.2 million in the three drilling fund loans we proposed."

"Good. I saw the envelope and thought you should open it. Sounds like we got what we need. Let's get the paperwork done. With this participation, we can attract other independents, other prospects. Excellent work. We'll both be rewarded if we can sign more of these deals."

Phil called JD's office. JD was out but his secretary promised to have him call back as soon as he returned.

That was the first of several drilling program loans. Money started rolling and the Oklahoma independent companies raked it in. The big gas production boom had begun.

Chapter 23

Charley came in from the supply yard, shaking rainwater from his coat and walking through Stephanie's open office door.

"We need to get our pipe yard leveled out, and some gravel added," he complained. "These rains on bare ground make a hell of a mess. Can't hardly load trucks or move material around in this mudhole. Plus, we need a retaining wall and gravel fill on the north end to level out an area that slopes down three or four feet, so we can add additional pipe racks on level ground."

"You're right, and luckily we just received some money. Your father called to say the loan money came in from the Chicago bank, and he's giving us $250,000 to fund our expansion and upgrade the yard and shop."

"Gre—wait a second." He leaned on her desk, his face inches from hers. "We're supposed to be equal partners in Sooner Oil and Gas, which means our half of that loan should be over $2 million."

"Now don't get too high and mighty," Stephanie replied sternly. "Phil asked for $5 million participation, but we don't know what he actually got. And remember, some of that money will come to us by way of material purchases, rental, and well service fees." She leaned back and lightened her voice. "I think this $250,000 is just for our overhead and expenses. I'm going to assume we can spend it as we please. Don't you think?"

Charley straightened up. "Are you sure? No strings attached."

"He said we'll get a check. I didn't hear any requirement to purchase anything specific. Guess we can spend it as needed."

"Damn, momma, I could jump over this desk and give you a big kiss. Baby gets a new pair of shoes, or Daddy buys a bass boat. This'll let us do more than just level and upgrade the pipe yard." He sounded like a kid telling Santa what to put under the tree.

"This is still loan money, not a gift," Stephanie warned. "We need to fix a few things around here and hire more hands to keep up with the increase in demand we'll get. Phil said two other independents are getting similar money from Continental. We should make them an offer to stock their pipe and tools. We can pre-order and have it here when they need it. Also, George Martin says Vinson will pay us to stock a limited amount of specialty casing inventory for them. Stocking charge for holding materials, or buying through us at an increased price. New sources of revenue."

"JD is a long way from starting that deep well. I understood the pipe for that well will be purchased out of the drilling fund. If this loan is separate, I can think of several things that fit me well."

"By the way, we got an invitation in the mail today inviting us to a party at Cowboys Dance Hall next Saturday."

"Really? From who?"

"One of your father's cronies, Cliff Culpepper, and his Ports of Call Oil Company. I called over to JD's office and learned it's expected to be quite a bash. Culpepper has rented the whole dance hall for this party. I'm guessing anybody who's anybody in the central Oklahoma oil business will be there—other independents, suppliers, rig builders, mud companies, you name it, they'll be there."

"Wow, sounds like fun," Charley said. "Did you tell 'em to count us in?"

"I did. It should be a good chance to meet Cliff Culpepper. He's going to drill a deep well in Caddo County, going for the Hunton sands below 15,000 feet. That's a multimillion-dollar project requiring hundreds of joints of drill pipe, casing, and services. We want to be their favorite supplier."

"Let's call Will and your mom to see if they're invited."

"I'm sure they are," Stephanie replied, "and I expect people from Oak Tree Bank, like Phil and Erin, are also invited."

"I met Cliff when I was much younger," Charley said. "Like Dad, Cliff scratched out a living hauling produced water in the late '60s with a trucking and service business like ours. He now owns several trucking companies, and he's drilled over one hundred successful oil wells. Some say he's worth a couple million. He owns a Lear jet and a helicopter he uses to take bankers and deep-pocket investors to his production sites to raise money for new drilling ventures. This deep well venture is beyond anything he's done. The riskiest and most challenging by far. For him, taking big risks has paid off."

"So far."

<><><>

The next Saturday, McCall's Production Equipment Company worked overtime to finish a big unit, a new gas separation unit designed by Will, for Phillips Petroleum. Business growth continued, straining their shop capacity and adding to an unresolved cash flow problem. Will came in from the shop to tell his mother they'd finished the job and it was ready to ship.

Johanna exhaled after a long drag on her Marlboro. "That's great. Your new product designs are a success. I'm proud of how you've expanded this company, building new products, for the past couple of years. Without those new products, we wouldn't be this successful."

Pleased she recognized his contribution to the business, Will gritted his teeth and held back criticism of her smoking. He and his sister thought she had kicked the habit months ago. It didn't last.

She leaned forward and snuffed out the cigarette in an already full ashtray. "In fact, I doubt our salvage business would have survived if you had gone back to school."

"Thanks, Mom. That means a lot coming from you. I'm happy we've done this together. Dad would be proud of us. I still want to talk to Phil about extending our credit limits. We need to expand to take advantage of the increased demand. The biggest need is a separate weld shop, making room in the main shop for more assembly and testing. We have room in the back lot where the trailer was. I'm estimating a cost of about $50,000, financed by getting an extension of our credit line or a short-term loan. It could be paid back within a year if business continues to grow."

"Yes, Will. We also continue to have a cash flow

problem that has taken our extended credit line to the limit. What if the boom fizzles out and demand falls? As the financial administrator of this company, believe me, I understand our ongoing financial squeeze. We've had this talk several times before and my answer continues to be no. I'm not going to get this company overextended."

Turning around, she picked up her cigarettes and pulled one from the pack to her lips. Will frowned as she snapped open the metal lighter. She stared back at him and stopped before the lighter flame touched the end of the cigarette.

"I know, I know. I've got to quit. Last week Dr. Blake told me if I don't stop smoking, I'll be dead within five years."

"The doctor is right, Mom. We're all concerned about your smoking, and we've heard that smoker's cough too many times. You've avoided cancer, but I bet that cough is a symptom of emphysema."

"Okay, you're right." She mashed the unlit Marlboro into the butt-filled ashtray, picked up the pack and tossed it into the trash can nearby, then opened the bottom drawer, pulled out a half-empty carton, and tossed it into the same can.

"Great, and I love you for trying to quit. But you've tried and failed this cold turkey method twice before. Have you considered getting the new Nicorette gum? I've read reports of its success helping people kick the habit. It gives you the nicotine without the harmful tobacco elements."

"That's a good idea. I'll try it. In the meantime, you and I need to continue managing the cash flow problem and avoid taking out another loan as long as possible.

If this deep gas drilling boom doesn't last, and business drops, we'll have enough problems with the loans already on the books.

"Besides, Will, you know the history of the oil business in Oklahoma. The boom-to-bust cycle has repeated itself many times since the first gushers at the turn of the century. Oil men of that time, Tom Slick, Henry Sinclair, Tom Cosden—they all made and lost fortunes. A philosopher once said, 'Those who don't learn from the past are doomed to repeat it.' Believe me, the bust side of the cycle is coming again. Let's enjoy the boom, operate within our means, and not get overextended."

Not at all surprised, Will respected her position and offered an alternative. "We could try for a cheaper solution of a concrete pad with a heavy temporary cover, enclosed with roll up walls. It'd be half the cost, and would work nine months of the year, all but the coldest when it'd be hard to heat."

"That sounds more doable. Go ahead, get it started. I'll get you the money from somewhere."

Will changed the subject. "I heard JD and Sooner got their big loan through Phil and Oak Tree with a big upstream participation from Continental Illinois Bank and Trust in Chicago. A sizable amount will flow to Stephanie and Charley for work and materials going to JD's deep gas well projects. Maybe we should ask them for a loan."

"Well, good for them. And no, we will not risk family relationships by borrowing money from them."

"I hear you, Mom, but I have to say, they're getting several hundred thousand dollars, which will burn a hole in Charley's pockets in a matter of weeks."

"You're right, Will, but that's their problem and I

don't want us, or this company, to get in the middle of the Arnold family business, personal or otherwise."

"I know you're right, again. On a different subject, did you see the invitation from Cliff Culpepper and Ports of Call to a party at Cowboys tonight? Christi and I are going, and we're going to meet Phil and Erin and Stephanie and Charley there. You're welcome to come with us. We're planning to make an appearance to meet Culpepper and maybe some others, but we won't stay too late."

"Yes, I saw the invitation, and no, I have no interest in loud music, drinking and dancing, or seeing Culpepper throw his money around. You all have fun. It'll be an excellent opportunity to press the flesh with potential customers."

Will and Christi arrived at Cowboys Dance Hall and stood at the entrance, waiting for his sisters and their spouses. The party was in full swing, with a local country and western band belting out an old country song by Hank Thompson.

"There's an old favorite that lets you know you've arrived at a honky-tonk," Will said. He attempted to sing a bar. "I didn't know God could make honky tonk angels. I knew you'd never make a wife. You gave up the one that loved you and went over to the wild side of life, or something like that."

Lines of urban cowboys and cowgirls gathered at the two open bars. Others mingled around the edges of the dance floor, dressed in western shirts with swinging fringe on the sleeves, faded blue jeans, and a variety of custom cowboy boots, like their own. Across the hall from the double door entrance a mechanical bull stood in a ring with padded mats on the floor so the wanna-be cowboys and cowgirls full of liquid courage could try their skill at staying on the automated wild ride for eight seconds. The aroma of cowhide leather mixed with cigarette smoke filled the hall.

Stephanie and Charley arrived with Phil and Erin in tow. After greeting hugs and kisses all around, Christi offered the first evaluation of the band entertaining the already a rowdy crowd. "That band is doing an okay job of Hank Thompson's 'Wild Side of Life.'"

Stephanie remembered a very similar song. "You know a rebuttal song was written to the same tune. It's called 'It Wasn't God Who Made Honky-Tonk Angels,' recorded by Kitty Wells. It was also big a hit."

Will led the group in. "Let's find a table before they're all taken. I'll bet there are a hundred people here, and it's still early. I see a few tables in the back. Follow me."

Charley said, "You all go ahead, I'm hitting the bar."

After claiming a table, the ladies chose seats and Will and Phil headed to the bar. They met Charley coming back.

"Go get a beer," he said. "It's an open bar and they've got just about anything you want."

Walking back to their table with longneck Coors in hand, Will and Phil approached a middle-aged man wearing a suede jacket over a silk tropical print shirt. A young blonde woman hung on his arm. Will recognized Cliff Culpepper in his signature outfit of Hawaiian shirt, dark slacks, and tassel loafers.

He offered his hand. "Mr. Culpepper, I'm Will

McCall. I think you knew my father, Lew, and our salvage equipment business. This is Phil Pederson, with Oak Tree State Bank. Thank you for the invitation to your party. It looks like great fun."

"Well, glad you all could be here. Yes, I knew your father and was sad to hear of his sudden death. Years ago, he and I hustled for nickels and dimes hauling water and doing what was necessary to make a living in this business. Have we bought any of your stuff lately?"

"I don't think so, but we just wanted to thank you for including us in your party," Will replied.

"Sonny Hunter is my production manager. He pulls together the processing systems when a well is completed." Culpepper looked around. "He's here somewhere. I'll be glad to introduce him to you."

Will thought a harmless story wouldn't hurt. "Thanks. I'd like to meet him. You may have purchased our tanks through contractors. My mother and I are running the business now, and we've added new separation equipment to our traditional refurbished tanks. We'd love to build you the gas treating unit you'll need when you bring in that deep gas well."

"Well, we'll see about that in six months or so. I think you're referring to the well we're about to spud in northern Caddo. It's going to be one of the deepest ever drilled in Oklahoma. It'll be called the Tomcat Number 1, and if all goes as planned, we hope to reach the Hunton sand before Christmas."

Phil spoke up. "That's impressive. As a banker, I'm curious about how you funded such an expensive project. Did you go through Penn Square Bank? Oak Tree has also written several large loans for independents planning similar projects."

"No. I've got working interest partners and a little bank funding. We're not doing a limited partner drilling fund, if that's what you're thinking."

"I understand; but if you ever need some extra funds, here's my card. We'd be happy to talk with you over at Oak Tree. And thanks again for the party. How late do you expect to keep it going?"

"The bands will play until two, or until everyone goes home. My group is taking the jet to Las Vegas at midnight. Stay as long as you like. Enjoy."

When they got back to the table with drinks, George Martin was there.

"Hey, George. Have you met everybody?"

"I know Stephanie and Erin, although it's been years since I've seen them, and I met Charley. I know his dad, JD—he's a good customer of our US Steel casing. You and Christi have been hiding from me. We should get together again soon."

"I expected to see you here, knowing you've sold casing to Culpepper."

"We have on several of his oil wells in Canadian County, but he hasn't ordered any for the deep well yet."

"Phil and I just ran into Cliff and Phil asked about his financing. Cliff said he has partners and isn't using a drilling fund to raise capital. Do you think he's financing most of the costs out of his pocket, or spreading the risk like most independents?"

"It's my understanding he has multiple partners," George replied. "He has two well-known investors, Ken Ellison and Buddy Appleby, who have years of experience raising money to drill holes in the Anadarko. He also got money from Washington Gas & Light in DC, a large utility company in need of natural gas supply to fuel their power plants. The utility made the major investment. I hear Culpepper, as the operator, has an 18 percent interest."

"A good strategy from Culpepper's standpoint," Phil said. "A low-risk share with enormous potential return, assuming the gas reservoir is as big as they think."

"I worked up casing design for the depth he's planning, below 15,000 feet," George said. "I'm hoping to show it to him soon. The design recommends a special high-strength, high-alloy P grade casing as he gets close to the bottom. About the time he calls for surface casing in a couple of months, he'll need to order the deep casing in order for it to be ready in time. It's not a stock product for US Steel. Plus he'll need premium joints to hold the high pressure he'll encounter at 15,000 feet."

Charley added, "This project will challenge Culpepper's methods of drilling and completing wells. He's a seat-of-the-pants operator when it comes to selecting casing and necessary mud weight to balance down hole pressure. His philosophy of cutting corners to minimize costs is a dangerous one. Quote, 'If you haven't had one or two kickbacks while making hole, you're not a very cost-efficient driller.' He also believes in perforating several pay zones at one time, to get the maximum short-term production. That shortens the life of the well and the total oil recovered."

George agreed. "Remember his experience, and your dad's experience, on shallow oil wells of three to five thousand feet drilled here in Canadian County and other fields like the Arkoma where Will worked one summer. The kickback or blowout risk on those is minimal compared to drilling into a natural gas pocket at 15,000 feet where pressures could exceed 10,000 pounds per square inch. I expect Ports of Call will buy medium N-80 grade casing for the intermediate section of the hole below the standard surface casing. They'll be sorry if they trust it to hold up under the higher pressures below 10,000 feet."

Will added, "The few deep wells drilled in the Anadarko Basin over ten years ago were expensive and dangerous but still very tempting for the high gas flow measured. Low gas prices made those earlier gas wells uneconomical. Today, with a price moving above seven dollars per thousand cubic feet, the return could be huge, with a payback in weeks, not years. But as George points out, the risk-return graph line is very steep."

Chapter 24

A few days following the Sooner loan approval and final signing of documents, George Martin got a call from Cliff Culpepper.

"Mr. Culpepper, I'm glad you called. I've been trying to get in to see you since hearing you're about to start a deep well in Caddo County."

"Yes, and I'm told Vinson has access to some proprietary high-strength casing joints designed for high-pressure deep wells."

"We do, and I'd be happy to come talk to you about the premium joints. I can also help you with your casing design, picking the right size and material at the top and at what depth you should switch to a stronger, heavy-wall design for the high temperatures and high pressures you can expect below 10,000 feet."

"Okay, good. Why don't you come over to my office and show me?"

"I'm tied up this afternoon, but I can be there tomorrow morning. How about 9 a.m.?" George asked.

"Tomorrow is good, but if you don't want to miss me, I suggest eight. I've got to leave the office by nine."

"Great. I'll see you at eight tomorrow."

George knew he had a tremendous advantage over other tubing and casing suppliers. Vinson was an exclusive distributor of US Steel casing and specialty joints designed to withstand the heavy weights and pressures of deep gas wells, from stainless steel alloys to chrome-moly, high carbon alloys for extreme conditions expected at 15,000-foot depths.

George could also calculate the most economical casing string design, selecting the casing at the top for holding the weight and the most economical depth at which to switch to an alloy material for resisting the high-pressure conditions at the target depth.

The next morning, George arrived five minutes early at the Ports of Call office building on the east side of downtown Oklahoma City. He parked on the street, entered the building, and took the elevator to the eighth floor. Lights through the glass front door showed Culpepper was in, but George saw no receptionist at the front desk. A few moments after knocking, an attractive young woman approached and unlocked the door.

"I'm guessing you're here to see Mr. Culpepper." She continued speaking while opening the front office door. "I apologize. I'm a little late today. He's usually here by seven, so I expect he's back in his office. Who should I say is here?"

George followed her in, introducing himself with a good morning greeting.

There was a shout from a back office. "If that's Mr. Martin, get him some coffee and bring him on back."

When George entered his office, Culpepper sat with his back to his door, wearing his silk Hawaiian shirt. "Good morning. I'll be right with you, Mr. Martin."

When he turned around, the receptionist was placing a mug of coffee on his desk. George, still standing, introduced himself and offered his hand. "I don't believe we've met, but I feel like I know you. Will McCall and I were roommates at OU, and you knew his father Lew McCall."

"Okay, yeah, another case of 'it's a small world.' Yes, I knew Lew McCall. We bought, sold, and traded used tanks when he started his business, and we were both trying to scratch out a living in the early '60s." Culpepper didn't get up as George approached but offered his hand in greeting.

"Please have a seat and tell me about Vinson and casing with special joints. I understand Vinson is one of the few suppliers of the specialty tubing and casing we'll need for the deep well we're about to drill in Caddo County. We'll be going for deep natural gas in the Hunton sand below 15,000 feet. The material grade I've always used is a J-55, which I'm sure you'll tell me is not strong enough. I've also run a lot of N-80 casing. What's the limitation to using it on a deep well?"

"You can use the N-80 grade for the intermediate string, and I've run a calculation that will optimize the depth at which you should switch to a stronger P grade to handle the higher pressure and temperatures below 13,000 feet. If you agree on the design, I'll send you a quote that will include the double-sealed specialty joints needed to hold the high pressures you can expect at 15,000 feet. We've shipped similar casing strings to other independents drilling for the deep gas."

"Nah," Culpepper replied. "I'm not concerned about getting a written quote; just call me with the numbers and I'll give you a purchase order number to work with. We won't need the surface casing for few weeks, and it'll take at least two to three months before we need the N-80. We might run it deeper because I know the P-grade is an expensive pipe."

"Just remember," George advised, "N-grade pipe might not handle the pressures below 13,000 feet. High temperature isn't the only problem. Add high pressure with high temperature and the risk of failure increases. Most stainless steel alloys lose strength above six hundred degrees. The P-grade alloy has more elements to strengthen the casing when both high temperatures and high pressure are present."

"Okay, good to know. Thanks for the education. Call me with the price for the complete casing string and I'll give you a PO. We're still taking in investors as working partners. Have any interest?"

"If I had a discretionary six-figure account, I might be interested. I'm not there. Maybe next time."

"You don't have to invest all in cash. Many are using a standby letter of credit for investing in these deep wells."

George knew all the risks and rewards of the standby letter of credit. "Yes, and I'm familiar with the tax benefits; but I also know the enormous risks with these projects."

"Ten years ago, I couldn't have risked drilling this deep," Cliff admitted. "The big rigs, casing materials, and heavy tools for this type of well weren't available. Only the majors had the deep pockets to absorb the cost and risk of drilling these deep wells. Now that stronger tools are available, banks and Wall Street investors are eager to make the investment, believing a big payoff is possible. We're having to hide behind trees to avoid the bankers trying to give us money. Even local banks like Penn Square and Oak Tree are funding these projects. If they're buying in, why not you? Anyway, let me know if you want in."

"I will, sir, and thanks for your time. I'll call you with the figures tomorrow."

George left Ports of Call offices excited at the prospect of a million-dollar pipe order, and remembered Will told him JD Arnold had leased a section in eastern Caddo County near the Culpepper lease. George headed to JD's office to propose a similar casing design. Luckily, he caught JD about to leave the office.

"Mr. Arnold, George Martin, Vinson Supply. Do you have a few minutes to discuss your casing program for your deep Anadarko play? Will McCall recommended I offer a casing design for that project."

"Yeah, he mentioned that to me, and I'm familiar with Vinson and your specialty casing, but I don't have time today. I've got to meet some people in Caddo County at a site we're trying to lease."

"I promise, this won't take much time. How 'bout I show you a casing design over a quick lunch, my treat. I know a great little barbeque place near Tuttle."

"Okay, I've got a thirty-minute drive and need to be there around one o'clock, so I'll drive my car."

George followed him out of the office door into the parking lot. "Shouldn't be a problem. I'm parked right here. Just follow me."

The barbecue lunch went well, and George got JD to accept a quote on a casing program George designed.

Then George risked a question he knew JD might dodge. "What can you tell me about these drilling leases? I understand they're getting expensive, and if Culpepper or you or others can complete a big gas find, I expect lease prices will skyrocket."

"Yes, they will. That's why I'm trying to buy leases in the Anadarko before they get too expensive. I'll buy the landowner's minerals if they're willing to sell. Most will if they don't need the money for retirement or their kids' college tuition. Buying the minerals is more costly than leasing, but it gives us more control without the time constraints of a lease. These deep wells take months to drill, so paying for a limited-time lease is risky. Also, the Oklahoma Corporation Commission's rules have a limit of one deep gas well per 640-acre section of land, and all the landowners in the section have to sign the lease terms before an operator can get a drilling certificate. All the landowners get the lease terms, driving the lease cost close to seven figures before you drill the first foot of hole. And with that, I've got to go, Mr. Martin. Thanks for the lunch."

"One last question, Mr. Arnold. Have you considered leasing any acreage in Grady County? I know the McCalls own property there that I believe is on the eastern edge of the Anadarko Basin."

"We have, and I talked to Johanna about buying her minerals. She wasn't interested. Maybe she's waiting to see if one of the deep wells in Caddo County is successful, which would drive up lease prices in Grady."

Chapter 25

On Christmas eve, Will and Christi arrived at Johanna's with the newest family member, Thomas Lewis McCall. After giving up trying to start a family early in their marriage, Christi found the right doctor to help her carry a baby to term.

She pushed Tommy in a stroller and Will carried two Christmas pies into Johanna's busy kitchen. The rest of the family was already there. Barbra Streisand's jazzy version of 'Jingle Bells' flowed from the stereo in the den.

"Merry Christmas, everyone," Christi greeted, with an echoed response from all. "I love that jazzy version of 'Jingle Bells' you're playing, but it would be even more fun if we were really dashing through fields of white, not in Oklahoma."

"Merry Christmas, Mom," Will said, setting the pies on the counter and walking across the kitchen to give her a hug. "It's been a while since we've all been together."

Stephanie approached, with Crystal and Donny. "Merry Christmas, Christi." She hugged her, then bent to say hi to Tommy. "Would you look at this sweet boy? You kids say hi to your cousin."

Will greeted his sister with a kiss on the cheek. "And look how Crystal and Donny have grown. Crystal must be in junior high, right? And Donny starting first grade?"

"Yes, the joy of raising a teenager has begun," Steph replied.

"Really, Mom!" Crystal said in a disgusted voice.

"I'm six years old," Donny said, proudly holding up the correct number of fingers.

"Six? Wow, you're getting to be such a big boy," Christi replied. "Where's Charley? He didn't come with you?"

"No," Stephanie replied. "He sends his regrets. He went over to his dad's to help with a problem."

"JD's not ill, is he?"

"Heavens, no. It's probably something those two are scheming about. He didn't choose to explain before he left."

Will, in a soft voice, said, "Mom, how are you feeling?"

"I'm fine. Merry Christmas to you, son!" she answered, then quickly turned away to cough. A deep, gurgling sound.

"That doesn't sound good, Mom. Didn't the doctor prescribe a different medicine?"

"No, he gave me the name of a company that rents oxygen equipment and said I should schedule regular sessions breathing oxygen every day to keep up my energy. We need to discuss the possibility of me dropping to part-time next year and maybe hiring a bookkeeper who could also serve as office manager."

Will agreed. "Do you have someone in mind?"

"How about Erin? I mentioned it to her, and she

showed interest in the idea. Her job experience indicates she has the skills. Think about it. I'd like to bring her in and explore the possibility. In the meantime, let's enjoy this Christmas with everyone together."

Christi picked up Tommy from the stroller when Johanna stepped around Will to reach them.

"I want to hold my newest grandson. You come here to your nanna." Johanna took Tommy, walked into the den, and sat down in her recliner.

Will walked to the other end of the kitchen counter where Erin and Phil were helping with dinner preparations. He gave Erin a kiss on the cheek and shook hands with Phil again, wishing both a merry Christmas.

"How are you all this holiday season? I hear the bank has been funding some big drilling projects— including a deep well drilling project JD is about to start."

"Yes, you heard right," Phil answered. "And our oil and gas loan portfolio is growing. We take an origination and service fee, and a large national bank takes the largest participation. We've signed loans amounting to over twenty-five million. This coming year, I expect to double or triple that amount, if the larger upstream banks continue with their participation in these loans."

"Phil's done well. He was recently promoted to vice president at Oak Tree, including a big bonus this year," Erin said proudly. "We've decided to invest in Sooner's drilling fund. They're raising money to take on a deep well project. You get a nice tax write off using a letter of credit, and if the well is successful, the return could be many times the original investment. Have you and Christi considered investing in a drilling fund?"

"No," Will answered. "We've got a home mortgage and I'm still paying off a note taken out to purchase the company stock. Christi took out a loan to start her own real estate brokerage business. So we're stretched thin, with little discretionary money right now. But congratulations, Phil. A well-earned bonus, I'm sure, and I hope the investment pays off."

"How is McCall's Production Equipment doing?" Phil asked. "I remember you had cash flow problems. Is that holding you back from growing? What you need is a sympathetic banker." Phil moved his hand to his pocket for his billfold and said with a wide smile. "Do you have my card?"

Will laughed. "Yes, I have your number, and we could use additional credit. However, Mom and I have resisted getting overextended with loan obligations. You never know how long this gas boom will last."

"I applaud your conservative mindset," Phil said. "There's still time. The deep drilling activity is just beginning. You heard about the recent blowout of the Tomcat well?"

Will nodded, and Phil continued. "I understand they got it under control and are drilling again to reach the Hunton pay zone, several thousand feet deeper. That brief incident gives additional credibility to years of speculation about the enormous amount of natural gas at that depth. There are thousands of greedy investors from all over the country who'll want a piece of the deep gas treasure."

Will switched the subject. "I'm sorry Charley and JD aren't here tonight. I was going to ask about JD's deep well project that Erin mentioned. I understand Oak Tree is raising money through a drilling fund. Do you know the status of the well? Has JD spudded it yet?"

A loud knock came from the front entry. Will said, "Who could that be? I'll get it." He headed toward the front door, with Phil following. When he opened the door, there stood Charley holding a grocery sack and Christmas presents.

"Charley, what a pleasant surprise. Merry Christmas. Come in this house."

Charley walked in and Phil stepped up. "Let me help you with that sack. I'm guessing it goes to the kitchen."

"Yes, thanks," Charley answered. "I'll take these gifts to the tree." He waved at the others in the kitchen, who shouted Christmas greetings.

"Can I get you a beer?" Will offered.

"Nah, I'm good for now. Maybe later."

Phil returned. "Will was just asking about your dad's deep well project. We knew the rig was on site. Have they started making hole?"

"That's Sooner Cat Number 1," Charley said. "It's about five miles southeast of the Ports of Call Tomcat well. They just spudded the well so they're months away from reaching the same target depth. When they've made a couple of thousand feet, we might go out and visit the site. Would you like to go along?"

"Definitely. I'm sure we'd both enjoy that if you can give us a day or two notice," Phil said.

"What about the Tomcat well?" Will asked. "Do you know any details about the recent blowout?"

"I heard it was a lack of mud weight. Culpepper had a big argument with his drilling supervisor, who, I'm guessing, wanted to switch to a heavier, more viscous mix that costs more money. Baroid, the mud supplier, has excellent mud engineers who'll calculate mix for your expected depth or pressure, but Culpepper has a reputation for ignoring technical advice and relying on his experience alone. Selecting mud or casing by a seat-of-your-pants method can be dangerous in a well expected to go below fifteen thousand feet."

After dinner, Will found his mother in the kitchen for a chance to speak to her alone. "Mom, didn't you say JD wanted to lease your property for a future well?"

"Yes, he called me about six months ago, wanting to buy my minerals. I told him I'm not interested in selling the minerals, but I'd consider a drilling lease. He said he was buying up minerals for future possibilities. Said he's trying to put together a lease deal with all the rights holders in the section. I said I'd talk to him when he got the others to agree. I expect to hear from him after the holidays to let me know the status. I'm planning to meet with Sam Buchanan and a landman after the holidays so I can better understand my options."

Will wanted to stay connected to his mother's lease negotiations. "Please let me know what you decide, or what the options are regarding a drilling lease. I'm just offering to help you if there are some issues or terms you might have difficulty working through."

"I will. Thank you, son, for offering to help."

Chapter 26

It was a chilly morning the last weekend in January 1981. Will was coming back in the house with the Saturday edition of the *Daily Oklahoman*. He pulled off the rubber band, tossed the paper onto the kitchen table and walked over to make a pot of coffee. Returning to the paper he pulled out the business section to catch up on the oil and gas news. There was nothing of note other than an update on the price of unregulated natural gas at eight dollars, fifty cents per thousand cubic feet.

The phone rang, and he moved quickly to answer it, hoping it wouldn't wake Christi. It was Stephanie.

"Good morning, Will. Did you hear the news about Culpepper's Tomcat well?"

"No. Did they reach the deep gas?"

"Yeah, and a lot more than they could manage. They had a catastrophic high-pressure blowout at pressures over ten thousand pounds. They were back in the hole with a new bit at 16,151 feet, continuing to drill, when a monstrous gas kick blew out the drilling mud, shale rock, and drill pipe through the crown of the derrick. They had a bunch of visitors, investors thinking about buying in, to see the big rig operate, and they all had to run for the hills."

"Wow," Will exclaimed. "I bet that mad scramble was a sight to see. And did you say joints of pipe? I know what a blowout is but exhausting the drill pipe is unbelievable. Anyone hurt in the chaos?"

"Luckily, no one was seriously injured. The shower of mud and rocks was followed by fourteen thousand pounds per square inch of natural gas exhausting into the air with an ear-piercing roar, creating a huge condensate cloud over the whole area. Someone compared the roar to standing near a 747 jet airliner taking off. They're evacuating the nearby town of Eakly for safety concerns. The gas flow was estimated at one hundred million cubic feet per day, and I'll bet it catches fire, if it hasn't already."

"Wow," Will repeated. "I just read the current price of the unregulated gas is $8.50 per thousand cubic feet. If the price continues to rise because of this big show, that well could return a million dollars per day. If you and Charley paid ten thousand cash and a letter of credit for a 1 percent interest, you could be rich. I just hope they can get the well under control."

"I'll remind you again. You and Christi could have made the same investment."

"It would have been difficult with our other debts. I'm happy for you and Charley. I believe Phil and Erin made a similar investment."

"Charley said the crews on the Sooner Cat Number 1 lease, five miles south of the Tomcat, can hear the exhausting roar of natural gas at their rig. Which reminds me, aren't you, Charley, and Phil planning to visit the Sooner Cat soon?"

"We're planning to go next month. Hopefully, they'll have the Tomcat under control by then."

GAS MONEY

<><><>

For the next several weeks, Culpepper, his partners, and contractors made multiple efforts to control the runaway Tomcat #1 well, including the drilling of two rescue wells to reach the original hole and shut off the escaping gas. Sparks from rocks thrown into the steel rig ignited the gas several times, only to be blown out by the spraying mud. The collapse of hundreds of feet of shale rock trapped heaving drill collars at the bottom of the string, making reentry impossible.

A pipeline company laid a surface line connected to the wellhead, but it could only take a fraction of the total gas flow. Interstate pipeline companies were on the sideline offering nine dollars per thousand cubic feet if Ports of Call could get the flow under control. Reservoir engineers calculated a total production potential of 100–200 billion cubic feet of natural gas. That would return Culpepper $200–300 million.

A 1 percent interest in the overall life of a big gas well was a potential fortune.

<><><>

While the efforts to control the runaway Tomcat well continued, Phil picked up Will and Charley and headed west toward the Sooner Cat lease in Caddo County. Will asked about the progress of the well.

"So, Phil, I'm guessing this meeting has to do with the bank's role in financing the project. I know it's none of my business, but are they having money problems?"

"I can answer that," Charley said. "They're having lots of problems. Lost circulation, mechanical failures, slow penetration due to rotary bit failures. They're burning through lots of cash, and they're behind schedule."

"Yes, that's the reason for the meeting," Phil added. "I'm expecting JD to ask for more money. How much and for what exactly, I don't know. But I'm also interested in seeing the operation. I know the drilling technology, tools, and machinery have changed significantly since you worked on a rig several years ago, Will."

They drove north on a county road then turned through a fence onto the temporary lease road. Bulldozed out of the prairie, it was covered with a bed of baseball-sized rocks, laid to withstand the weight of heavy trucks hauling the rig machinery. On the fence post at the entrance to the lease was a metal sign reading *Sooner Oil and Gas LLC, Sooner Cat #1 Lease.*

Phil's Suburban crested the top of a small hill a mile or so from the fence line. The massive drilling rig suddenly appeared in the distance. The superstructure of the rig was as large as a two-story building. It held up a colossal, one-hundred-foot-tall derrick. The overall size dwarfed the drilling rig Will worked on in the summer of '69.

"Wow, that rig is bigger than I imagined," Will exclaimed.

Phil's Chevy continued rolling over the rocks, generating a vibrating road noise.

Suddenly Will shouted, "Phil, stop the car."

Phil braked firmly and the Suburban bumped along the baseball rocks to a stop. Will watched the massive drilling rig lift the deep string of drill pipe out of the hole. Without the road vibration noise, it was unusually quiet except for a different low roar in the distance. It was easy to assume the source was the big rig pulling the drill string.

"Is that roaring noise I hear coming from the rig?" Will asked.

Charley said, "I think that's coming from the Tomcat blowout five miles north of here. It's still exhausting gas at tens of million cubic feet a day."

"So why aren't we hearing the Sooner Cat rig pick up the drill string?"

"Because the Sooner Cat is operating on electric power."

"Unbelievable," Will said. "They're picking up hundreds of tons of drill pipe with electric motors? I was listening for diesel engines revving to pick up the drill string. In the sixties, it took two big diesel engines to pick up the drill string, and they made a roar you could hear for a mile."

Phil put the car in gear and continued the drive up to an office trailer located half a football field away from the rig superstructure. When they got out, Will heard the distinctive electric motor *humm* coming from the drilling rig.

JD stepped out of the trailer, greeted Phil, and thanked him for making the trip. He also shook hands with Will and Charley as they expressed superlatives describing the size of the rig and overall operation.

Will asked about the silent operation. "Charley says you run this with electric motors. I sure would like to know the details and the source of the power."

"This rig is designed to run totally off electric power. The hook load, or maximum lifting load, is 1.5 million pounds, powered by two 1500-horsepower GE direct-current motors. We pull high voltage AC electricity straight off the power grid. High voltage lines bring power from a nearby substation to the rig's electric panel, which houses a rectifier that converts the AC to DC current to drive the big motors. The panel also serves as a distributor of conventional AC electricity to other small pump motors and rig lighting."

"Impressive," Will remarked, "but isn't that electrical power more expensive than the traditional diesel engines? I would think the cost of diesel fuel is lower than electricity. Or is it more expensive to connect enough diesel engines to get the same power?"

"My engineers did an overall cost analysis of different power options, and they determined electrical power was cleaner and less expensive, with far less maintenance cost."

"I didn't know that size DC electric motor exists."

"The crew is pulling the drill string for a bit change. We've encountered hard rock for the last couple of weeks and have lost our mud circulation twice. We'll put on a new hybrid design that has a secondary layer of cutters. That should allow us to get through this hard rock section faster."

JD was explaining the drill bit trip change they were in the middle of when a man in coveralls and a hard hat entered the trailer.

"Meet my tool pusher, Steve Ratcliff. I've asked him to give you a tour, Will, while Phil and I do business. Charley can sit in with us."

"Will McCall?" the man in the coveralls said. "The college man who used to run back-up tong on the Brushy Creek many years ago?" He reached out to shake Will's hand.

"Well, hello, Steve," Will said, taking his hand. "It's been a long time. You're looking good. I guess you've graduated from derricks to management!"

"I'm on the rig floor now, but a manager I'm not. Come with me. I'll show you what a real drilling rig looks like today."

Will followed him out the trailer door.

<><><>

JD led Charley and Phil into a small office at one end of the trailer. "Phil, we're going to be short on drilling funds, and I'm hoping you can help us out. This deep well venture, like all the others, is draining our drilling fund faster than expected. We'll run out of money before we get to the pay zone. Then, when we do hit the deep gas, we'll need to add processing units and pipeline tie-ins. Can you help us out?"

"I don't think there's a problem raising more money. We have banks and investors lining up at our door for a piece of the action. How much do you need?"

"With no major upsets or delays, we should be near the pay zone in eight to ten weeks. After that, adding the cost of setting final casing and tubing, plus tying in a pipeline, we're going to need another five to six hundred thousand dollars."

"Okay, I've got a standard commercial loan form we can use to write this up." Phil pulled the form from his briefcase and began filling in the details. He asked another question related to costs. "Is this enough to cover your final casing order? I understand the final deep run is necessarily an expensive high-strength P-grade alloy."

"It should, and just so you know, I ordered it from Vinson, through Will's friend George Martin."

"George told me about the casing collapse that contributed to the problems of getting the wild Tomcat well under control. Ports of Call's choice of casing may have contributed to the well blowout. The casing collapse and broken drill string likely trapped the heavy drill collars, creating an impenetrable steel plug at the bottom of the hole."

"I think we're using the right grade. Plus, we won't skimp on mud weight, which may have been another factor in the blowout and the resulting casing collapse on the Tomcat."

"Again," Phil said, "money isn't a problem. Don't cut corners trying to save a few thousand bucks. If the big gas is there, it won't be a problem to pay it back. Let's just get you another million. That should cover your operating expense and the casing upgrade. I'll make the term six months, which should give you ample time to complete the well and ink a sale contract with a pipeline. More funds will be available depending on a strong well test. If there are unforeseen delays, we'll just rollover the interest and extend the loan period. Does that sound fair?"

"Hell, yes. More than enough. Don't you need some additional capital or in-ground reserves for loan back up?" JD asked.

"Nah, no worries," Phil replied. "We've got your file with your asset and reserves. I'll write up something that should satisfy our loan committee at Oak Tree." He finished filling in the seven-figure dollar amount and pushed the paper over to JD for his signature.

"We might have to adjust the interest to satisfy new money, but this amount is not unreasonable added to the five million already invested, so I don't expect any major adjustments. What production flow are you expecting?"

"Based on what we saw from the Tomcat blowout, I'd say, conservatively, ten million cubic feet per day initially, or approximately $2.1 million per month; and with luck, that number could double to $3 million per month. The life of these gas wells is much shorter than an oil well, but I'm guessing it could bring in $75–$90 million over three years, assuming the natural gas demand continues and the price averages $7 per thousand cubic feet."

"I wouldn't be surprised," Phil replied. "We continue to see strong demand. We're adding millions a month to our oil and gas drilling loan portfolio. This additional loan is small in comparison to other loans of this type."

As Phil added his signature, he said, "I'm approving this loan as I have for others of similar amounts, with no problem getting participation from the upstream banks. If there's resistance to final approval, I'll let you know. If our big bank participation holds up through the year, we might book $200 million in loans by the end of 1981. So what about all the gas? Are the pipelines buying it? Are long-term take-or-pay contracts still being signed?"

"Yes and no. There are big offers at prices approaching $9 per thousand cubic feet, but they're only good if the produced gas is from a formation below 15,000 feet. At higher depths, say 13,000 feet, where the Tomcat experienced a large gas kick, only an intrastate pipeline can purchase at the unregulated price, and those smaller in-state pipelines serve a limited market.

We need the interstate system that can handle the big volume we expect to achieve."

Charley spoke up for the first time. "Many of the current deep well ventures are just beginning. It'll take six months to a year to reach the Hunton sand. But we're less than a month from the Springer sand—where the Tomcat first blew out—and if we find gas there at a more manageable pressure and volume, it's possible we could have a gas well flowing fifty million cubic feet per day, producing an income of $10 million a month. Sooner Oil and Gas's share could be two million per month. You've got a piece of this, don't you, Phil? One percent interest could return a hundred thousand dollars per month."

Phil was saved from answering by the arrival of Will and Steve back from the tour, still talking about the big rig's tremendous capabilities. Instead he said, "Fellows, we need to head back. I've still got to get to the bank before closing."

They all proceeded out of the trailer and stood at the Suburban saying their farewells when the low roar from the north died down.

"Whoa," JD said. "Did you hear that? The Tomcat well just went silent. You suppose they got that well under control? If so, that's huge. It has the potential to generate over a billion dollars in revenue over its life, and the price of natural gas and drilling leases will skyrocket in the coming months."

<><><>

Will learned later that Culpepper had not gotten the Tomcat well under control. The roaring noise stopped because the well collapsed on itself, shutting off the blowout within seconds. During the following weeks several efforts to drill rescue wells failed, and it was widely reported the partners and contractors spent nearly $20 million trying to save the well. The one million dollars a day return they expected was never realized.

The enormous show of natural gas below 16,000 feet was confirmation enough to drive the wellhead price from $7 to $10 per thousand cubic feet. The higher price fueled a rush to tie up thousands of acres of drilling leases in the Anadarko Basin counties. Pipeline companies offered take-or-pay contracts, meaning they would pay for the full amount of contracted gas even if the pipeline wasn't able to take it. Banks and private investors continued to pour tens of millions of dollars into deep drilling ventures.

Alas, there was never another strike as big as the Tomcat, and by early 1982 the euphoria was waning. The wellhead price dropped, pipeline companies stopped signing big contracts, and suppliers like Vinson knew their best year in history was unlikely to repeat itself.

Part III
The Bust

Chapter 27

Spring 1982

Frank Wilson answered a call from John Littleton at Continental Illinois Trust one afternoon. "Good morning, John. How's everything in Chicago?"

"Cold and windy, normal for Chicago. I'm calling with an urgent request. This'll put you on the spot without warning, but I have no choice. Bank examiners from the Comptroller of the Currency are pressing for more documentation on in-ground reserves to support the oil and gas loans on the books, so we need more documentation on the loans we've extended to your oil and gas customers.

"Also, it would help if you could bring the interest payments up to date. I'm told there are hundreds of thousands of dollars of interest in arrears on loans from your bank that we participated in. Many of these loans are being classified as substandard, which will require documentation to maintain capital requirements. The first oil and gas loan we participated in from your bank, the Sooner Oil and Gas Drilling Fund, is one of those we need to get up to date right away."

"John, I understand. In a few days, I'll be in a much better position to give you what you need. Our customer is aware of the need to complete the documentation on the in-ground reserves that support the original loan. I wasn't aware the interest payments were in arrears and will investigate that right away. I'll be able to make a complete report in a few days. In addition, our officers and board are trying to increase our reserve capital to add support to these loans. I should be able to give you a status on all of this by the end of the week. I'm confident we'll able to clear all this up."

"I'm not sure I can hold the examiners off that long. Do what you can and get back to me as soon as you have something solid."

Frank hung up and immediately asked Ms. Sunderland to call Phil to his office.

"Yes, sir, right away."

Within minutes, Phil knocked on his boss's open door, then entered. "What's up?"

"Come in and shut that door."

Phil did and then took a seat in front of Frank's desk as his boss got to business.

"I just got off the phone with John Littleton," Frank said. "The Comptroller of the Currency is questioning their oil and gas loans from banks in Oklahoma, including Oak Tree. The issues center around a lack of complete documentation and overdue interest payments. I'm not shocked by the incomplete documentation, but now we've got to produce additional assets to support the loan amounts."

"Well, we knew the operators were light on documentation, but Continental approved the loans with what we submitted. They were looking at the enormous potential and didn't hesitate to offer participation at whatever level we recommended."

"Yes, the large banks and investors were willing to assume the risk and approved whatever we asked for. We thought the biggest issue would be keeping up with interest payments and didn't concern ourselves with the real value of their collateral, their in-ground oil reserves. If Continental decides to call these loans, we could be in trouble."

"I understand. We need to review our complete portfolio of oil and gas loans and identify the ones lacking the necessary reserves or capital to support the loan."

"Start with the Sooner Drilling Fund loan. Contact JD Arnold and press him to get their asset documentation up to date and make their back interest payments. I don't care if the interest payments come from unspent loan money. And we need documentation of the collateral assets originally promised. He needs to understand that Continental Illinois is being pressed by federal examiners to show how the participation loan is backed. Otherwise they'll classify it as troubled, meaning Continental could show up on our doorstep to review the loans and borrower in detail; or worse, call the loan."

"When reviewing the whole portfolio," Phil said, "we could package solid loans with weaker ones to make the package more attractive to sell. Selling a few of those loan packages would reduce our exposure."

"Good idea. I'll get you some help from a couple of the other loan officers. Meanwhile, I'm going to contact some other large banks to see if they'll purchase part of this loan, as well as some of the smaller drilling funds, to reduce our portfolio. Do you know what our total loan portfolio has grown to since last quarter?"

"I'd estimate it's over two hundred million. Up to half that could be in trouble because of the drop in the price of natural gas. That threatens the borrowers' ability to pay the loans back, even if they complete the wells and sell the gas."

Later that day Frank called the vice president of the energy division at Seattle First and offered to bring him some drilling fund loans he thought they'd be interested in. "I'll be glad to fly up there and bring these to you for your consideration later this week."

"Your call is interesting since I received a similar one from John Littleton at Continental Illinois a few days ago. My answer to you is the same one I gave John. We're not interested in loans that have insufficient documentation, that aren't performing, or that examiners have classified as troubled. Our portfolio already has tens of millions of dollars in poor performing oil and gas loans to Oklahoma oil and gas operators, and our auditors have said absolutely no more. We have to reduce our exposure to the Oklahoma oil and gas activity in any way possible. Would you like to buy some of our smaller deals? We can make them attractive to a small bank like yours."

"Thanks, anyway," Frank said. "We're trying to reduce our overall portfolio, as well." He thanked the VP for his time and hung up.

The call and rejection added to his concern. The Sooner Oil and Gas Drilling Fund loan originated by Oak Tree was only one file out of several file drawers of outstanding loans to drilling funds, independent operators, rig builders, and pipe suppliers. He stood and leaned with both hands on his desk, stunned from the immediate turn of events, and muttered under his breath, "We're going to be in big trouble if we can't sell some of these loan packages, unless some of these projects get completed soon."

Phil, Bill Sellers, and a few other loan officers started packaging the smaller loans for sale. Bill was totaling the outstanding loans still open after two years of writing loans everyone expected would be a growth bonanza. The tab of Oak Tree loans was already well over $200 million, with many more files to review.

"We're going to sort these according to our own evaluation of their credit worthiness," Phil said. "We need to evaluate each client, starting with those we believe are solid, with documented reserves and making timely payments. A second group will be modest risk, those with solid backing but no success or payments. The third group is the riskiest—insufficient documented reserves and no payments on interest or principle."

Bill Sellers added, "We should also arrange each group by size of the loan. We can package a good performing loan with one or two loans from the other groups, or two solid small loans with two of the riskiest. Then we can decide where to unload the packages. In fact, we could offer each package to multiple large banks and take the first reasonable offer."

After two hours of pulling folders and sorting out the loans as, they had reviewed most of the files and put them into the class groupings.

"The overall total without an accurate audit is $265 million, plus or minus," Bill announced.

Chapter 28

Phil decided he should tackle the first big loan he was part of signing and had a personal connection with. He drove directly to the C&S Trucking office, which was used as the headquarters of Sooner Oil and Gas.

Luckily, the receptionist said the three principals were together in a meeting and escorted him to a conference room.

"Hey, Phil," Charley greeted as Phil entered. "What brings you in today?"

"Good morning, everybody," Phil replied. "Good to see you all. Sorry to interrupt your meeting."

Phil shook Charley and JD's hand and acknowledged Stephanie seated at the far end of the table with a nod. "I'm glad you're all here because I need your help on the drilling fund loan. As you know, we sold participation in that big loan to a larger upstream bank, Continental Illinois Trust in Chicago. They're pressing us for the documentation on the reserves and assets originally promised to back these loans."

He looked JD in the eye as he continued. "They took our word—your word—of adequate assets after submitting a bare-bones outline of current holdings, operating wells, and in-ground reserves. Now, they're getting nervous because those assets were the minimum to secure the initial loan and lacked the backing of specifics such as reservoir engineering reports. Since the Sooner Cat well is taking longer to complete, costing much more than predicted, they're asking for more details and more assets."

"They know these deep gas wells take months to complete," JD answered. "They knew the risks and should know there are always unforeseen problems with any project of this size. You know we'll get there."

"JD, we were out there months ago extending you another million dollars, and you still haven't reached the pay zone. I'm sympathetic, I know how tough it is; but these big national banks don't care. Like the loan sharks in the movies say right before breaking somebody's kneecaps, it's not personal.

"I don't mean to make light of the situation, but we're near that point. We've got to show Continental Illinois details of enough assets to back the Sooner Cat Fund loan or they're going to call it. Also, they want you to pay the accrued back interest. I know you haven't spent the money on rigs and tools or piping because none are available. Don't you have some cash left for interest payments?"

Stephanie interrupted. "Phil, C&S Trucking is part of Sooner, and we have some cash. What's a minimum interest payment that would buy us a few weeks until JD's well comes in?"

"You need to pay the interest in arrears. Sooner owes for two quarters last year and one this year. At the contract rate, that's about $90,000."

Stephanie stood up from her chair, arms out wide and jaw dropped. "You mean we owe $90,000 in unpaid interest?" She looked over at JD. "I thought we were making quarterly payments. Didn't you make interest payments last year?"

Phil answered before JD could speak. "Our records show you'll soon owe four quarters worth of interest. There was no pressure to collect for the second quarter this year because we all expect your deep well to be producing soon, which should allow you to pay interest and some principal this year."

Now leaning on the table, Stephanie turned again to JD and Charley on the other side. "I warned you big spenders, this is not free money. We can't just blow it on cars and boats waiting for the well to come in."

She pointed to JD. "And you went on buying up leases to tie up valuable locations, and now we're overextended. It doesn't take a financial wizard to know if you can't get that damn drill bit into the deep gas pretty soon, we could be finished before we ever sell the first cubic foot of gas."

"That's not true. You're overstating the problem, Steph," Charley replied. "We have assets we can liquidate for the short term until we get into production."

"You mean sell your boat, that chrome-plated off-road pickup, and mortgage the property? Sure, we might cover the back interest. Then how do we pay the current interest while we're waiting for the big strike?"

JD also offered a solution. "Phil, at the time of the original loan, your bank and the Continental people took our word on the in-ground assets. We can revalue our in-ground reserves at today's prices. That'll raise the assets and should calm the fears of the big bankers. Tell them to be patient. Give us a little more time. We're still going to make 'em rich!"

"Well, maybe. You're thinking the high price of gas that's tripled, but much of your reserves are oil and it hasn't risen that much," Phil warned. "And, the price of wellhead deep gas is falling. If the Sooner Cat well doesn't come in soon, there won't be enough money to pay your debts, let alone make anybody rich."

"If we pay the back interest from last year, $60,000, that'll buy us some time, right?" Stephanie asked. "I can have a check for you tomorrow."

"It'll help if you can pay that. More would be better. We'll try our best to hold them off a few more weeks."

"We have the cash; we're just holding it for unexpected expenses," Charley said.

"Great. I need to get back to the office. Steph, call me tomorrow when you have a check ready. I'll be glad to come by and pick it up."

<><><>

After Phil left their office, the three principles of Sooner Oil and Gas looked at each other with stares of disbelief. The reality of impending financial ruin was out in the open. It had been in the back of their mind for weeks, stifled by the delusions of the big payoff they'd get.

"Where the hell are you going to get sixty thousand dollars, Stephanie?" JD blurted out.

"When Charley rushed out and bought his chrome-plated rock crawler and the bass boot with the drilling fund money, I transferred eighty thousand into a separate account for just this type of problem. It doesn't cover all the back interest, but maybe it'll be enough to take the pressure off for a while, till we can figure something out."

JD barked back at her. "You don't have to pay that much. They won't call this loan while there's still the prospect of a big return. We'll keep making hole and get that well completed. In the meantime, let's get the value of our properties, our original collateral, upgraded, using the current price of oil today. We haven't evaluated them at the higher oil and gas prices that went into effect a few months ago. Our CPA should be able to help. If the wellhead price holds a few weeks longer, we'll be fine. Oak Tree just wants current documents, however written, to ease the pressure from their big participating banks. The new valuations will give them confidence their loan is safe."

Chapter 29

Two days later Phil stopped at C&S Trucking to pick up the check Stephanie promised, then went on to the bank. When he arrived, the tellers were busy so he headed for an open counter to fill out a deposit slip. The counter was in the center of the main floor and as he pulled out a deposit slip, he noticed unusual activity. Employees moved about quickly, talking quietly to each other. He completed the slip and took the endorsed check behind the teller's counter to one he knew.

The teller asked him, "Mr. Pederson, is the bank in trouble?"

"In trouble? What makes you ask that?"

"A group of men in dark suits arrived this morning and went straight to Mr. Wilson's office. A few minutes later, they all went upstairs to the boardroom. I've seen bank examiners before and that's what those guys looked like."

"I'm sure it's just a routine visit. They like to make a dramatic entrance, even when there's not a problem."

Turning toward his office, he realized the call Frank got from Continental Illinois had been a red flag, a precursor to a visit from the bank examiners. As he walked calmly to his office, he deliberately avoided looking up at the board room windows.

He dropped his briefcase in his office and strolled across the banking floor, passing Frank's empty office, to stairs leading up to the second floor. The curtains on board room windows were closed.

When he reached the back stairs, he took two steps at a time. At the top of the staircase, he knocked, then opened the board room door to see four strangers in dark suits on one side of the table, with Frank, his secretary, and Bill Sellers on the other. A tall stack of files sat on the table, and a finance clerk stood aside, holding more files.

"Phil, I'm glad you're here," Frank said. "Bill, would you go down and handle daily operations while Phil and I work with these gentlemen?"

As Bill walked out of the room, Frank introduced Phil to the group. After a handshake the head examiner, introduced as Mr. Ebert, began explaining their purpose for being there.

"Phil, as I was explaining to Frank, we're making a spot examination of your oil and gas loan portfolio. We've completed an overview of just a few large loans so far, but I can tell you that some of them should be classified as substandard or doubtful. I can see by the sheer number you've been successful in signing that we'll be here a few days to review them all."

Phil's mind raced. What can he say? Frank wouldn't even look at him.

I'll just listen and agree. Promise to gather better documentation and collect back interest payments. Save the good news for last. The payment we just received from Sooner might give them confidence that we can get these problem loans in shape.

Mr. Ebert continued, "Meanwhile, we'll set aside

those that might need further review or a change in classification. I suggest you review the collateral and terms with the intent of either raising more capital or finding other buyers for these poor performing loans to lower the bank's total portfolio amount and avoid a financial crisis for the bank."

Phil looked over to Frank, expecting him to respond. His boss sat stoically with a blank expression. That was surprising. The guy that led this aggressive loan program—including the participation strategy with the larger banks—was going to leave the job of cleaning up the mess and pulling the bank out of financial trouble to Phil.

"We have brought some large loans into compliance, as you recommended," Phil replied. "Today I deposited a large interest payment from Sooner Oil and Gas, and they're working to establish the current value of their in-ground reserves and bring their loan documents up to date."

A different examiner spoke up. "Mr. Pederson, payment of back interest is of little help when there's insufficient in-ground reserves to support the original loan amounts."

Probably a junior examiner, or apprentice, with his ill-fitted suit and clip-on tie.

"I understand," he said. "In many cases, the issue is simply incomplete documents, not the lack of assets. Plus, the value of those assets, the oil reserves, has risen since the big bank approved the loan. We're also working to move these local loans to our participating banks in Chicago and New York. We'll do what's necessary to get the questionable loans supported and loan payments up to date. We request time to get the questionable loans into compliance, and we'll offload the smaller loans to improve our reserve capital."

Mr. Ebert spoke again. "Look, gentlemen, you have an urgent asset problem. The value of in-ground oil and gas reserves is dropping. That means your clients need to find additional assets, or you need to sell or call some loans to reduce your unfunded liability."

Frank stood suddenly. "Phil, you work with these men today," he said, "and later we'll go over the loans that need additional support. I'll work on raising our capital reserves. I'd appreciate a preliminary report of your findings of major problem areas. I'm confident we can resolve some of the questionable loans during your review process."

"Of course, Mr. Wilson. We'll report daily."

"Great, thanks." Frank shook Mr. Ebert's hand and hurried out of the room with his head down.

He's feeling the pressure, too. How deep is this exam going to go? The Sooner Cat needs to find the big gas soon. Or figure out some way to make principal payments on their loans. Otherwise, the FDIC will take over. That can't happen.

The junior examiner cleared his throat. "Mr. Pederson, we're also looking into the finances of the officers of the bank, and I can start with your account. It includes two large loans, a mortgage, and a refinanced personal loan, plus a letter of credit that exceeds your listed assets by almost $10,000. Your personal loans, like the oil and gas loans, are part of the bank's liabilities exceeding capital limits, and like them, you have thirty days to either list additional assets, raise additional capital, or supply income sources that will support the interest payments plus an amount of principal, or else they'll call these loans to reduce the bank's liabilities."

This made Phil wonder if Frank was in a comparable situation. His extended credit line or outstanding loans could be a million dollars, or more.

Phil excused himself and returned to his desk, leaving the examiners to continue going through loan files. He would get back with Bill to help review the loan packages, but he needed a moment to calm down. Bill could continue to package the smaller loans for now.

An hour before the bank closed, Phil got an internal call from the front customer's desk. "I have a Mr. Arnold here who says he wants to talk to you right away." She added in a whisper, "He's not very happy."

"You can send him back. He knows where my office is."

When JD approached, Phil was opening the door, ready to greet him.

"What the hell is going on?" JD asked.

"Come in, JD," Phil said, and made sure to close the door behind him. "What's the problem?"

JD plopped into a chair. "This damn bank bounced my check, and when I called to question why, I was told they froze my accounts pending the bank audit. I know auditors don't shut down the bank for their review, so what's going on? I've got suppliers all over me for overdue invoices. I need the cash in my account."

"Continental Illinois Trust, our participating bank, raised a red flag because the price of wellhead natural gas has been dropping, causing many oil and gas loans to be reclassified as doubtful. Most are nonperforming, meaning no interest or principle has been paid. You happen to be the principal owner of one of the largest loans. As I told you and Charley and Stephanie the other day, we need to identify more assets to relieve the pressure from Continental—and our own bank examiners."

JD made no response so Phil continued, "We're also trying to sell some smaller loans and find more investors who'll purchase stock in the bank to increase our capital reserve, to stabilize our balance sheet. I'm in the same boat as you. The examiners want more assets and up-to-date reductions of my loans, or they'll freeze my accounts, too."

Without me spelling it out, he should realize his company and personal credit are one of many in trouble, Phil thought. *The only thing that can save him is his Sooner Cat #2 well. It needs to strike gas now.*

He asked, "What's the status of your Sooner Cat #2 well? Into or close to the pay zone? Just a show of gas, even if it's not from the deep zone, will relieve the pressure coming from the banks. I warned you this squeeze was coming. No lender will mark time forever. We never told Continental Illinois the first Sooner Cat well failed. Since you skidded the rig and went back after the same deep zone last summer, you're still not close to striking the deep gas. Without a strike, or additional collateral, and soon, they'll call the loans. In your case, we've stretched the value of your assets and in-ground reserves to the limit, so it's going to take a major strike to get them off your back."

"We're close to hitting the big, deep gas. I'm not going to try to produce at a shallow level just to grab a minor amount of production. Reaching the Hunton sand in a few days will be worth it. We'll just slow-pay our suppliers and utilities until then."

Chapter 30

A month later, Phil was in his office early with loan folders stacked on his desk. He leaned back in his chair wondering what size discount terms would make the loans attractive to other banks.

His radio nearby was playing a popular song from the '70s appropriate for the day and once again Phil was singing his version.

"There's a calm before the storm that's been comin' for some time. When it's over, I know they say, it'll rain on a sunny day. I want to know, have you ever seen it rain, every seen it rain, on a sunny day?"

Word was out in the banking industry about the risky oil and gas loans hitting the secondary market. It was imperative to unload the nonperforming loans before examiners or the FDIC declared them worthless, which could lead to Oak Tree's insolvency.

At eight thirty, he walked out of his office to get another cup of coffee and saw Frank hurrying across the bank floor, headed toward his office with Ms. Sunderland following. She struggled to keep up, juggling her notepad and an armload of papers. Frank's quick steps and concerned face meant trouble.

From his office door, Phil noticed a crowd forming outside the bank's front door. It wasn't unusual for a few people to gather outside before the bank opened, but today at least a dozen people were twenty minutes ahead of the bank's 9 a.m. opening. It was an unusual and concerning scene. It reminded Phil of pictures of the run on the banks during the Depression.

His office phone rang, and he went back in to answer it.

"Mr. Wilson is requesting all management staff to meet in the conference room in fifteen minutes, unless you are engaged with a customer."

Phil grabbed his notepad and walked across the bank floor to the boardroom. Bill Sellers met him at the stairs to the second floor.

"What's this about?" Bill asked. "We're not in trouble because of the oil and gas loans we're holding and can't get rid of, are we?"

Phil let the sarcastic question go unanswered as they entered the room and selected chairs near the head of the table. Other commercial loan officers were there, staring at Phil and Bill without a word.

Moments later, Frank entered the room. "I know we're all busy, so I'll make this short. You know our oil and gas loan portfolio is under pressure from the examiners, who have classified some as nonperforming. We're talking to those customers hoping to raise more capital and offering some of their loans to other larger banks at substantial discounts.

"In the meantime, I need your help to assure our customers the bank is not at risk of closure. We are not insolvent, and their money is safe. I'm confident we will work this out soon. We're trying to sell the nonperforming loans and, with the support of our auditors and legal team, I can assure you we'll do whatever's necessary to get these issues resolved and our loan portfolio back within our capital limitations. Please continue to communicate my confidence in the bank's financial standing and assure customers their deposits are safe. Do not elaborate on any details. Our loan issues are serious, but manageable. Thank you for your help and support as we get this resolved. That's all."

Phil stayed as the others left the room. He needed to talk to Frank about his efforts to unload some of the classified loans. "Phil, let's go to my office and you can tell me about your calls to the upstream banks."

In Frank's office, Phil explained his conversations with Continental Illinois, Michigan National, and Seattle First about buying some of Oak Tree's questionable loans. "I'm not finding any interest in buying our loans, so we need to group these classified loans with some good performing loans to make the entire package attractive. Maybe start with Chase since they haven't taken large participations like Continental and Seattle. The other issue involves documentation. Continental Illinois didn't sign some of the original participation loans. I have our loan clerks pulling together the drilling fund loans, like the Sooner Drilling Fund. We need to clean up the document deficiencies the examiners have identified."

"You're right." Frank said. "Why don't we go to Chase in New York, then to Chicago. We'll meet with John Littleton again to clear up documentation and offer the loan packages. I'll set up the meetings and Mrs. Sunderland can make the travel arrangements for Thursday."

In New York they met with a low-level Chase VP who

took a ho-hum attitude to this local state bank bothering him with a small loan package. Luckily he accepted it. Phil figured he was unaware of the examination going on in Oklahoma City.

They flew on to Continental Illinois in Chicago, where John Littleton had agreed to meet. Frank and Phil sat in a familiar conference room and were pulling files from their briefcases when John arrived.

"Gentlemen, welcome back." They exchanged handshakes and small talk before he moved to business. "I know you've brought some documentation on the original participating loans that needs to be completed. If you have new documents, I'll see that we complete our records, and we'll return the originals. I'm sure that's not the main reason for your visit, though, since we could have done this through certified mail."

Phil responded, "You're right, John. We're offering some smaller loans in packages that we can discount. They're not high risk, just loans we need to get off our books to get under our reserve capital limits. We offer the package for a single purchase, and we're willing to negotiate terms attractive and profitable for Continental."

"Under normal circumstances, we'd probably be a buyer," John said, "but we had a call from the Controller of the Currency recently warning us about oil and gas loans originating from local Oklahoma banks. They mentioned Penn Square and Oak Tree by name, among others. They identified three loan classification, at risk, doubtful, or a loss. Due to their warning, we'll require additional scrutiny on this package, and we'll need full documentation on collateral, be it in-ground reserves or capital backing, and performance to date. I'm sure you understand. The best I can say is that we'll look at your package and get back to you in a few days; but given the business atmosphere you're in, with so many nonperforming loans in your state, it's doubtful we'll be a buyer."

Chapter 31

Phil and his fellow loan officers labored for the next two months packaging loans and offering them to large national banks in New York, Chicago, Michigan, Washington, and California at significant discounts. They returned to Oak Tree after unloading over $200 million worth of loans and were enjoying a few days of success when the bank examiners returned. Ms. Sunderland escorted the lead examiner, Mr. Ebert, and two junior auditors to the upstairs conference room and offered coffee.

Frank Wilson called Phil to his office to alert him of their arrival and tell him they'd be in the conference room. Phil entered Frank's office carrying files of the many loans they'd moved off Oak Tree books.

"What should we expect from these guys today?" Phil asked.

"That's a question I can't really answer until we get in there. I'm hoping your report of moving millions of loans off our books will relieve their scrutiny a bit. We still need to build up our capital reserves, and I'll continue to work on that side of our balance sheet. Mr. Ebert is your basic bean counter—he'll make decisions in a black and white manner. Which simply means this bank is still at risk. Hopefully, your work and some additional capital will hold them off for the near future. We'll go meet with them, and then I'll leave and let you report your success. I've got to get out a report to our board on our progress toward increasing our capital reserves. Come back to me after your meeting and we'll discuss our next move." They picked up the files and headed to the conference room.

"Mr. Ebert, gentlemen, welcome back to Oak Tree Bank," Frank said upon entering the room. "I think you'll be happy to see the progress we've made to improve our balance sheet. Most of the loans classified as substandard or worse have been sold, significantly reducing liabilities. Phil Pederson is here to report on his work to move poor performing loans off our books. I'll get back to you later today. Is there anything you need or questions I can help with before I turn it over to Phil?"

"I think the first item on our agenda should be to hear that report," Mr. Ebert said. "At the end of our last session, Mr. Pederson and his team had the tough job of getting your classified loans documented, sold, or otherwise collateralized. I can tell you we've examined several banks since then that were involved in poor performing oil and gas loans. Many of them are not likely to be open at year end. We look forward to Mr. Pederson's report."

"I'll leave you in Phil's capable hands, and I'll get back to you later when you've completed your review." Frank left the meeting knowing he would not be returning that day.

Oak Tree's board of directors had asked Frank for an update on the bank's exposure above its loan limits. Frank reported on Phil's work to package and sell nonperforming loans that were a major cause of the bank's liabilities exceeding their capital limits. He informed them of the need to increase the bank's capitalization and recommended an offering of bank stock to attract new investors and capital, but omitted the fact that Continental Illinois pressed for additional collateral and documentation on the drilling funds loans.

For the next three days, examiners pored over the updated loan files and the bank's balance sheet. Frank did not return for a status report that day because he was on a chartered jet to Chicago to meet with John Littleton. He hoped to get Continental Illinois to invest in Oak Tree stock, adding to their capital reserves.

Rather than meet at the bank, Frank invited John to dinner at the Chicago Hilton a few blocks away.

"Thanks for meeting with me, John," Frank said as John joined him at a corner table in the hotel restaurant. When the waiter arrived at the table, Frank ordered a Scotch and soda and a shrimp appetizer.

John said, "I'll have a Beefeater martini on the rocks, please." Then he turned to Frank. "I expected Phil to be with you. In any case, I hope you're here to report good news on our participating loans."

"Phil and our loan committee are doing an excellent job updating the required documentation and reevaluating the collateral reserves based on increased oil and gas prices. They've also been successful in moving many of our nonperforming loans to other banks. My reason for this trip has to do with our need for recapitalization, as our loans and extended credit lines have exceeded our bank's limits. One solution is to bring in more capital through the sale of stock. Continental could help us by investing in our bank, thus helping to keep us in good standing with the FDIC and Comptroller and securing the drilling fund loans we hold until the wells can produce gas and generate income. I wanted to get your thoughts before making a formal request, since I know you'll need to take the proposal to your board. What do you think?"

"Frank, I understand your problem and sympathize. I'd like to help, but I doubt we can get approval for what you're asking. We received notice from the Comptroller that our participating loans from your bank are in trouble. I was hoping for good news, such as a well strike, to get us both out of hot water. What's the status? I heard Sooner had given up on their original deep well venture but moved the rig to back down to the same sand formation, and that they were close."

Frank tried to put a positive spin on his answer. "We still believe that's the best solution, and there have been some gas kicks, showing that there is gas down there. They believe they'll strike big gas soon. We're talking about as much as thirty to fifty million cubic feet per day. At the current price of $8 per thousand, that would generate an income of $6–9 million per month. It would pay the loans back, with interest, within the month."

"Continental Illinois is also under considerable scrutiny due to our large portfolio of loans to the deep gas drilling ventures in Oklahoma. Most of them are at risk, like yours. If we didn't know the examiners were in your offices, we'd be there asking for the same documents and capital support. We'll both be in trouble if some of those Oklahoma deep gas wells don't come in soon. It's possible that the Comptroller and FDIC will force us to take over Oak Tree, or that the other upstream banks and Continental will take over your bank as a joint venture. There's talk of creating a federal entity called the Resolution Trust connected to the Federal Reserve Bank to assume assets of several banks headed for insolvency."

They tried to finish their dinner on a positive note, both sympathetic to the financial squeeze they were facing. Frank returned to Oklahoma City late Friday empty handed and called Phil at home that night. "Phil, I just got back in town. Have the examiners completed their work?"

"They're finished, and we're waiting for a formal report, but the news isn't good. We haven't unloaded enough loan packages and continue to be in jeopardy. I'm afraid the examiners will report about $20 million in contingent liabilities beyond our limits. No other bank or investor will touch our stock."

"What about us, the officers? Any report on our stock or accounts?"

"Nothing formal. I also tried to get a reading on whether individual investments, by me or other officers of the bank, in the Sooner Drilling Fund are a conflict of interest, or if we'll be able to sell our bank stock to satisfy the letter of credit loan to Sooner."

Frank didn't confess his comparable situation, knowing his credit line and loans from the bank exceeded two million. Without new capital, the Sooner Cat well would have to strike a big reservoir soon if they were all to survive.

For the next two weeks, they put more effort into resolving the loans in trouble with more documentation, stretching valuation of assets, and agreeing to substantial write-downs. No one, including

John Littleton at Continental Illinois, thought the bank would be insolvent, but the month of July 1982 proved them wrong. Oak Tree, Penn Square, and many other banks in Oklahoma closed.

Chapter 32

August 1982

The next month Stephanie sat in her office looking for a way to keep Sooner Oil and Gas from bankruptcy. The Sooner Cat well reached the deep Hunton sand zone but produced only a minimum show of gas, not enough to justify production. Sooner debts were growing by the millions, many times their assets.

Her office phone rang, interrupting her concerning thoughts. It was Charley, and Steph spoke before he could. "Where are you? We need to figure out what assets we have left, not committed to the drilling fund loan, that we can protect from bankruptcy."

Charley's reply was matter-of-fact. "I'm over at Dad's office. We've decided it's a losing proposition to fight this bankruptcy. S&C Trucking and Arnold Drilling company are both responsible for the outstanding loans since we're both part of Sooner Oil and Gas, LLC. Our attorney says the LLC charter shields our personal liability."

"Maybe" Stephanie said. "But you can bet they'll call our personal letter of credit, and the bank will liquidate the assets to pay the loan."

"I'll be home later, and we can talk," he answered, "but I'm sure we're screwed. It's time to get out of town."

"We're not leaving," Stephanie said. "You better get your butt over here now. You and I are in this together. I'm not letting you bail on me and the kids, and we're not riding your father's coattails. I'm betting any plan he has in mind is about saving his own ass, not ours."

"We can't see any way except to take what cash we have and leave town," Charley replied. "Dad has some cash stashed away and says we should leave the state, maybe head to California, and start over."

"What do you mean *we*? No, damn it!" Stephanie said. "I am not running away. We're not following your father to California. Why California? You and I will work this out together when you get home." She slammed the phone down.

It was late when Charley showed up at home, stumbling in from the garage. "Steph, I'm home," he shouted. She met him in the kitchen.

"Keep it down. The children are asleep." She paused, watching him shuffle to the sink to fill a glass of water and pull a bottle of aspirin from the cupboard.

"You're drunk. You've been to Junior's, trying to drown your sorrows, haven't you? Or trying to pump up your courage to face me? Well, you're going to be glad you're numb when I kick your ass. What makes you think running away will solve our financial problems? Until we get them solved, they'll haunt us wherever we go. So, we'll file for Chapter 11 bankruptcy. In Oklahoma, they can't take the house. The law protects our domicile. We can find jobs until we pay the debts and get our credit back."

"Maybe you can. I'm not going back to driving a truck for five bucks an hour," Charley said. "Dad has some cash, and we own our vehicles. We can go with him and Julie to California and start over. He says Culpepper went out to his home in California to avoid his creditors, too. We could establish residency in California. Otherwise, we'll both be in bankruptcy, hounded by creditors every day. If you stay you can have the house. Sell it for whatever equity there is."

The shock from his cowardly desire to leave, abandon her and the children, turned surprise into anger. "I've had it with you. You'd rather grab a few bucks and bail than take care of your family." Her voice cracked and tears welled up in her eyes. "You'll abandon your family just to save what little lifestyle you think you have left?" She left the kitchen, retreating to their bedroom.

He followed, insisting they had another option. "You could help us stay by getting some money from your mother. She got paid big bucks for a drilling lease on her land."

The accusation stunned her. "How do you know that? Who told you she leased her land for drilling?"

"Dad told me she leased her mineral rights after the Tomcat strike, when the lease prices went up in Grady County. I don't know what she got, but some leases sold for three thousand per acre. She could've gotten over two hundred thousand dollars to lease her eighty acres. Hell, some properties in Caddo County got nine thousand an acre."

"You don't know that for sure, and besides, that's her business. If it's true, we can ask her for help, if we stick together as a family. Filing Chapter 11 bankruptcy and consolidating our debts might allow us to save the business. It wouldn't be easy, but we could start again."

"Easy to say, but not reality." Charley walked past her, pulled a suitcase from the closet, and started packing. "This oil and gas bust will last for years. Like I said before, I'm not going back to living in a two-room shack driving a truck for minimum wage."

Stephanie realized nothing she said would change his mind. "You goddamn coward."

When Charley looked up from his suitcase, her right hand caught him hard on the side of his face. She hurried to the bathroom, determined not to let him see her cry.

Chapter 33

Charley and JD left town the next day and a few days later Stephanie contacted a divorce attorney to understand her options for separation or divorce. The following Saturday, she called Erin to discuss her situation and strategy before attending the family Sunday barbeque at their mother's.

"Erin, I'm so sorry to hear about the bank's failure. I know it's hitting you and Phil extremely hard, and I'm sorry to burden you with my problems. But Charley left with JD, gone to California to avoid the company debts that are forcing us into bankruptcy. I'm calling you to see if you'll support a plan to get back our shares in the McCall family business that we got when Dad died. It's a chance for some income until we can get back on our feet."

"You're going to ask Mom and Will to give us back shares in McCall's Production and Equipment? What makes you think they would do that?"

"Dad willed us shares in the company when he died. I'm just going to ask to buy back my original shares for what I sold them for, but I need your support. Together, we have a better chance of making a deal."

"It would great for us if they agree but I'll be surprised if they do. I'll support you to a point, but

I won't jeopardize family relationships, or my self-respect. I won't stoop to begging."

"Okay, just nod in agreement when I bring it up tomorrow at dinner. I'll make the pitch."

Stephanie arrived at her mother's house at about five o'clock the next afternoon wearing a flowered peasant blouse, faded jeans, and her favorite ostrich quill boots, one of a few luxury items of clothing she could hold on to. She walked around the house to the large flagstone patio, where the large oak tree behind the garage provided shade. Will was lighting the charcoal in the Weber grill.

"What's for dinner, Chef McCall?" Stephanie asked.

"Hi, Steph. Well, I have some ribeye steaks from Harden's Meat Market and some hamburger patties for the kids. You brought 'em, didn't you? Where are they?"

"Donny went to a sleep-over at a friend's house and Crystal took a babysitting job. She needs the money for clothes and personal extras I can't afford anymore. I shared with them our money issues. They know there won't be any extra money for clothes, dates, or dinners out from now on. They'll have to earn their own spending money."

"Charley and JD running off really upsets me," Will said. "Running away to California is not escaping their financial obligations, but it is abandoning their family. I want you to know Christi and I are here for you, and we'll help you any way we can. We grew up with no extra money and managed pretty well. We can do it again."

He pointed to an ice chest next to the back door. "There's beer on ice in there. Help yourself, or you can fix a drink in the kitchen."

Stephanie was pulling a longneck beer from the ice

chest when Christi walked up. "Hi, Steph, it's good to see you. Did I hear you say the kids didn't come?"

"Yes, I'm enjoying getting away by myself."

Christi looked past her to Will. "Your mom and I are going to fix a salad. Let us know when you're ready for the meat."

"You got it, will do."

She turned and walked toward the back door, passing Erin coming out.

Will waited until she was closer to ask, "How are you and Phil doing? I'm sorry to hear about the bank going under. That was a shock to all of us. Does he have any job prospects?"

"Are you kidding?" Erin answered. "Half the banks in Oklahoma are losing money or insolvent because of the oil and gas bust. Hundreds, if not thousands, in the banking business are being laid off."

"I know you can get through this," Will said. "Your best assets will always be your education and your work experience. You both have real world skills to offer. You'll land on your feet. It'll just take time."

Erin responded with a sarcastic tone. "Right, time we don't have. We don't have any income, and what savings and the stock we owned they took when they called our letter of credit."

Stephanie listened to Erin refer to "we." *For me there is no we. Charley ran away leaving me to deal with all our financial problems alone.*

Watching Erin pull a beer from the ice chest, Stephani said, "Yes, we all have our problems. You know, when Charley ran away to California to escape our debts, the last thing he said to me was, 'I'm leaving and I don't plan to come back to Oklahoma. The house is the only thing left; it's yours.' So I filed for divorce and learned that the mortgage on the house is in Charley's name. My name is not on the deed. When we built it on JD's land I wondered why I didn't sign anything. I was so happy to move out of that shack we were renting, I didn't question it."

"Oh, my goodness!" Erin exclaimed. "Phil and I got scammed the same way because we didn't ask enough questions when his parents loaned us the money to buy our house. Phil's mother's name is on the mortgage with Phil's, not mine. Believe me, we've had some difficult arguments over how we can get the title away from his mother."

Stephanie said, "I called Sam Buchanan, and he says that under the community property laws of Oklahoma, half the house is mine, regardless of who's on the deed. He's helping me file suit to gain full ownership. Then I plan to sell it. After legal fees and closing costs, I might clear close to seventy thousand. That'll be enough to purchase a smaller three-bedroom house for me and the kids, and have a few dollars to spare. Assuming, of course, we can find buyers in this depressed economy."

"I had no idea how similar our situations are," Erin said. "When I got Phil to explain our finances, assets, and debts when the bank closed, he admitted his mother's name was on the deed because she loaned us the down payment. Now we're having to fight his family to replace her name with mine. They have financial problems, too, and don't want to give up the equity in the home. If we had thirty thousand, we could buy her out. I guess we need to talk to Sam, too."

The exposure of common financial problems motivated Stephanie to make her pitch to her brother.

"Will, you could help us by selling Erin and me back our shares in the company Dad gave us when he died. His will said specifically he wanted McCall's Production Equipment Company to be owned by McCall family members."

A stern look settled on his face and Will replied, "Yes, and I believe his wishes were followed."

Undeterred, Stephanie continued. "Erin and I once owned shares that Dad willed to us, and those shares could provide income now when we need it. I'm not asking you to give them to us. I'm just asking you to sell them back at what you paid. We'll give you your money back and you return the shares Dad gave us. I can pay part with equity from the sale of the house and the balance in time."

She looked over at Erin for support but saw her turned away. Not surprising. Stephanie knew Erin was embarrassed about her struggling marriage that included meddling in-laws to the point of financial collapse, all from chasing the big gas money.

Will didn't reply, but she noticed the muscles in his jaw tighten. She knew him well enough to know his anger was building.

Christi broke the tension when she stepped out the back door with the steaks. "These are ready to put on the grill." She set the platter down on a small table and looked at Will. With a puzzled expression she then looked toward Stephani, who turned away. Without another word to either, Christi walked toward the back door saying loudly, "The salad will be ready in a few minutes."

Will said, "Thanks, Christi, I'll put these on right away."

Stephanie received a glaring stare as he walked to the ice chest. She stayed quiet.

He pulled out a beer, opened it, and took a big swig. Walking back to the grill, he began calmly laying the steaks over the fire.

"Steph, I'm sympathetic to your situation, and I'll always be there for you and Erin—but not this way. Thirteen years ago, you and Erin didn't want any part of the dirty old salvage company and needed money. I borrowed money to purchase your shares when the company was struggling to make a profit. The share price reflected the company's financial condition at the time.

"You wanted the cash to start a new business you were sure would bring more financial benefits, more wealth, than a struggling tank salvage business. I'm sorry it didn't work out as you expected, but I feel no obligation to sell back my shares at the 1969 value."

Stephanie turned, walked over to the trash can, chugged the last swallow of her beer, and threw the empty rattling into the aluminum can. She walked slowly back toward the grill with hands on her hips.

Will continued when she returned. "Since then, and with Mom's help, those shares are worth at least three times what I paid you because I turned the salvage business into a manufacturing business with higher profits and far more potential than when you sold out. If I gave you and Erin your original shares back, I'd be giving away one-third of the profits of a much more successful company."

Stephanie was not going to give in that easily. "You take all the credit and brag on success, but admit it, you risked it all by gambling on getting some of the deep natural gas money like the rest of us. I know you lost money investing in with JD and his deep drilling operations. Plus, your business is way down, so the share price would be much lower than it was six months ago."

"What we do with our money is none of your business. And, yes, business is much slower today. We're surviving because we didn't borrow to expand our shop or load up on inventory as many did during the boom. We're not carrying a large high-interest loan requiring big quarterly payments, which is one reason your C&S Trucking went bankrupt."

Stephanie couldn't hold back, though she knew she should. In her desperation to get back to the lifestyle she had become accustomed to, she was willing to risk breaking a lifelong sister-brother bond.

"Admit it. You gambled more than your lunch money on the big gas play. You signed a letter of credit to Oak Tree just like we did, and lots of others who are now facing bankruptcy. You need our money to keep the company from going under."

"No company money was used to invest in drilling funds. Have you talked to Mom about this? I bet not. I know what she would say!"

"No, but I do think she's made money from leasing this land," Stephanie said. "Charley said she sold a drilling lease on this acreage, so she's got money that could help us buy shares back."

They all turned around at the sound of the back door slam shut. Their mother walked toward the patio carrying a large bowl of salad. Christi followed behind her.

"Whoa there, you two! Slow down," Johanna scolded. "Stephanie McCall Arnold, what did you just say?"

Before Stephanie could gather her thoughts and respond, Johanna continued, "It sounded like you're getting into your brother's business and my business. I heard you referring to a lease of this land's minerals. To be clear, I turned down JD's offer to buy my mineral rights long ago. I did enter into a lease agreement, but I won't go into details except to say I do have money that I can use to help you and Erin financially. That will not include trading shares of McCall's Production Equipment Company."

After a pause for a long, hacking cough, Johanna went on. "Secondly, you're wrong if you think the company has invested in a drilling fund, or any other risky drilling venture. I managed the financial side of the business and I assure you the company has not invested money in any drilling venture. Our business is way down, but we're not strapped with a high-interest loan with a big monthly payment."

When she stepped next to Will, she lowered her voice. "She's wrong to get into your business, but I'm concerned if you and Christi are also in financial trouble. Do you two need financial help?"

"Christi and I have financial issues and some disagreements regarding investments, none of which are causing us serious financial trouble, and we're working it out. It's no one's business but ours."

Until now, Erin had been quiet. She spoke now in a somber tone. "Mom, Steph and I need help to get back on our feet. We hoped to fall back on Dad's expressed desire for the company to stay in the family and sustain us all. We've got financial problems, and the business looks to us like the one vehicle that could save us. I'm willing to lend my skills to earn some shares, and I believe Steph will do the same."

Stephanie caught Erin's raised-eyebrow stare hinting for her to agree. She chose not to respond.

Johanna did. "I'll discuss this with you and Stephanie separately later. Will and I are running a business that looks nothing like your father ever imagined. The world, especially the oil business, is undergoing a slow time, with more tough times ahead. I'm concerned and sympathetic to your financial situations, but Will and I are responsible to the company and its employees. Company funds or shares won't be used to assist any personal financial problems. I love you all, I'm committed to this family, and I promise I'll help each of you with your financial issues. We'll get through this together. Enough for now. Let's enjoy the evening together."

Will turned back to the steaks and Johanna led Erin and Stephanie to help her set the patio tables. Christi stood by Will quietly mentioning one more important fact.

"I don't think I ever told you about the title search I did after our discussion of my purchase of the land west of here. I don't own the mineral rights on the eighty acres. They weren't included when Dad purchased the land back in 1969. They're owned by your mother."

Chapter 34

Johanna knew she must keep a rescheduled appointment with her doctor. Stephanie and Erin grew more concerned every day about her smoking and the ugly sounding, more frequent cough. Erin agreed to meet her mother there to have a second set of ears and ask questions Johanna might not think or want to ask.

"Good morning, Mom. I'm calling to let you know I'm about to leave home for Dr. Blake's office. How are you feeling this morning?"

"I'm fine, dear. I'm making coffee and will eat a piece of toast. Depending on traffic, I should be there in about thirty minutes."

"Good. I'll see you over there."

They both arrived to find the doctor was, of course, behind schedule. They waited another thirty minutes before he called Johanna in and began a routine exam, drawing a blood sample, listening to her heart and lungs, running an EEG, and taking a chest x-ray because of her history as a heavy smoker. He led her to the x-ray room and left. She returned to the exam room when the technician finished. The doctor returned later, carrying her x-ray films.

"Your blood pressure is a little high, but your heart sounds good. The chest X-ray is a little more concerning."

Doctor Blake turned on a lighted film viewer on the wall, attached the films, and motioned them to come forward. He pointed at the film with his ballpoint pen.

"If you look here, you can see a dark spot in the lower quadrant of your left lung. We'll need to do some additional tests to confirm what that is. With your history of smoking, it could be a malignancy. We'll do a biopsy, and if it comes back positive, we'll need more tests."

"Positive? You mean cancerous?" Johanna asked.

"Yes, but likely treatable. We'll check some of your lymph nodes for more signs. The lymph nodes act as filters and often catch cancer cells trying to spread to other parts of your body. Finding no cancer cells in the lymph nodes indicates any cancer is local and could be removed."

Dr. Blake took her arm and led her back to a chair. He spoke calmly. "I'm sorry to alarm you. A biopsy test is routine for an accurate diagnosis. Don't be too concerned until we get the results. And, even if the test is positive, most lung cancers are now treatable in various ways. My nurse will help you find a date to do the biopsy. We'll have the blood results when you return."

Erin and Johanna left the office, walking quietly to the car. Johanna said, "Now, I don't want you to be worried about me. We all know I've been smoking far too long, and I've had my chances to quit. I shouldn't be so shocked, but I am. You never think it will happen to you. Plus, I know other women that are doing well after surgery and/or radiation treatments. I'll be ready for whatever I need to do."

Erin put her arm around her mother and changed

the subject. "Let's get some lunch and a glass of wine. I can use one."

They went to a favorite Italian restaurant in South Oklahoma City, ordered two glasses of chardonnay, and split the lasagna with two salads and garlic bread.

"Tell me, Erin, how are you and Phil doing since the bank filed for bankruptcy?"

"Mom, you don't need to hear about our problems. There are moments I want to feel sorry for myself, but we went into this with our eyes open. We assumed a sure thing and ignored the risks, expecting a big payoff. It just didn't happen. You know the saying about hindsight being 20/20. No one expected the chain of events and market forces now pushing banks and investors into bankruptcy."

"I'm glad to see you're being honest with yourself and facing reality. My concern is your future. How is Phil doing? Does he have any job prospects?"

"Frankly, no. He may have to look out of state. His father can't help. First City is laying off loan officers and vice presidents. It's rumored that over a hundred banks in Oklahoma may go under because of the number and amounts of loans in default."

"Financially, what can I do to help you get on your feet?"

"We need to get title to our house away from Phil's mother. I called Sam Buchanan and he can help us but we don't have the money to pay him. Furthermore, Phil and I invested in the Sooner Cat #1 Drilling Fund through a letter of credit. We lost some cash, and the bank creditors called in the letter of credit, which took our CDs and stocks. We have some savings and equity in our home, but the bank won't give us a break on payments or allow us to refinance. We've got to keep up payments or we could lose the house."

"Okay. I'll take care of Sam's fees, and I'll cover your mortgage payments while you and Phil get jobs. Will your savings be enough to cover your bills for a couple of months?"

"Yes, thank you, that's a big help. We have enough for monthly needs for a while."

"Your sister is having similar financial problems with her home, and I'll give her similar financial support. In the meantime, you both need to find a job to help with those monthly bills."

She paused when the server brought their order, then continued. "The company has some long-term loans we've been carrying for some time, backed by our fixed assets. We avoided taking out short term, high-interest loans, so if we can continue to bring in some business, we should be fine. That's why I shut off the argument over the company shares. Will is still paying on loans to buy company shares from me, you, and your sister. He's the big reason we've been able to grow the business over the last thirteen years. So I can't support a plan to give back those shares at anything less than current value. I also know you and Stephanie don't have that kind of money. We'll have to find our way through this. We're still a family and families stick together. Your brother agrees and I believe he'll help during these tough times."

<><><>

Johanna returned the following week for a biopsy and

the removal of lymph nodes from under her arm and neck. Erin and Stephanie accompanied her.

Dr. Blake was prompt this time. "Good morning, Johanna. Erin, Stephanie, I'm glad you're here with your mother." The sisters looked at each other with silent anticipation, then at their mother, who outwardly remained calm.

"Johanna, the news is not good, but we have several treatment options. The biopsy on the spot in your lung came back positive. Also, we found cancer cells in your lymph nodes, which is more concerning. We must assume the cancer has spread. We'll want to do a CT scan to see if that's the case."

"I was afraid that's what you would find," Johanna said. "Now what do we do?"

"There are several treatment options." Dr. Blake said. "I recommend you see an oncologist to help us decide on a course of treatment. I've contacted Dr. David Baumann, one of the best oncologists in Oklahoma, to examine you and the test results. After we get his evaluation, we'll decide on a course of treatment. His office will contact you to set up an appointment."

Erin squeezed her mother's hand.

Stephanie asked, "Dr. Blake, what are her chances of beating this?"

"I can say with confidence, the treatments I think Dr. Baumann will recommend can be effective and extend a cancer patient's life for years. But cancer is difficult to cure. We celebrate when it goes into remission, and many patients live years in remission."

Before Johanna met with the oncologist, she had a CT scan, and the results were sent to Dr. Baumann.

When she met with him, she immediately insisted on getting a complete report, good or bad.

"The CT test shows tumors in your liver and kidneys," Dr. Baumann stated. "Removing those tumors will only remove the cancer in those spots. Unfortunately, they are a confirmation that the cancer has spread to other parts of your body. Chemotherapy is the best treatment regimen for attacking cancer throughout the body. I'm sure you've heard horror stories about chemotherapy, but you should know that each person responds differently."

"Will I lose my hair and be sick every day?"

"There's no way to predict the extent of side effects you'll have. Everybody's different. You'll need a two-hour infusion treatment each day for three days. Then there's a recovery period of two weeks before the next series of three, and six three-day series spread over four months. It's a grueling schedule, especially for anyone over sixty years old, but we've been able to put this type of cancer in remission in most cases."

Johanna was already steeling herself mentally to contend with the mountain of chemotherapy treatments and their known debilitating side effects. The doctor gave her a pamphlet explaining more than she ever wanted to know.

"When do we start?"

Chapter 35

Johanna completed six chemotherapy treatments over the next four weeks and struggled with violent vomiting, crushing headaches, and a weakness that left her unable to get out of bed. When she recovered her strength enough to insist Erin take her to the emergency room, Drs. Blake and Baumann arrived to see her within an hour. The ER doctor had drawn blood for analysis and her oxygen level was low. Both doctors recommended delaying further treatments until her red blood count and strength recovered. The chemotherapy had halted the growth of the tumors, but damaged her organs.

Stephanie and Will arrived at the hospital in time to hear the doctor's reports. Along with Erin, they gave words of encouragement and offers to help in any way possible, but Johanna shook her head.

"I'm sorry to disappoint you all. I'm too tired and weak, and don't think these treatments are effective enough to stop the cancer. The chemotherapy is killing me faster than the cancer. I want to go back home and enjoy what time I have left with you all and my grandchildren."

She agreed with Dr. Baumann's recommendation to stay in the hospital a couple of days to gain some strength before going home. Erin and Stephanie arranged for a hospital bed to be set up in her bedroom at home and found a home health group that would provide daily nursing care.

On the day of her scheduled release, Dr. Baumann came in to check on her and bring results of her most recent blood tests. Erin was there to listen to his report and help with the discharge paperwork. Stephanie waited in the car at the hospital entrance.

"Your white and red blood cell counts improved, but the CT scan taken yesterday shows we did not measurably shrink the tumors from the last treatments. Of course, stopping the treatments will allow the cancer to grow, but we will continue to manage your pain to keep you comfortable at home."

"How much time do I have, doctor?"

"It's impossible to say with any certainty. Each patient's general health and ability to continue to fight the cancer is different. In your case, without treatments, my best guess is two to three months."

Johanna looked over at Erin and said, "I have no reason to be shocked. You kids have warned me about my smoking for years."

She watched Erin's eyes fill with tears. "C'mon, Mom. Let's go home."

The orderly arrived with a wheelchair and in a matter of minutes Erin had her in Stephanie's car on the road home.

Having decided her fate, Johanna turned her attention to Erin and Stephanie and their financial problems.

"I want to hear from both of you how you're coping with your financial problems. After the arguments at our last family dinner, I promised to help."

"Mom, I'm sorry I pressed for the company stock," Stephanie replied. "It was poor judgment and I regret it. We got ourselves into these problems because of ambition and greed. We thought we were going to strike it rich. Now we're paying the price for risking it. Your help getting the house back in our name and picking up some mortgage payments has been a life saver. We're both picking up the pieces and moving forward."

"You know I love you both very much, and I'm proud you're determined to get back on your feet; but Will and the business need help too. He has to find a replacement for me; and Stephanie, you could help. I know you've been doing the administration work at the trucking company. It can't be that different from my job at McCall's Equipment. I'm confident you can step into my role."

Erin joined in. "Mom, Phil is looking for a bank position out of town. There's no chance of him going back to his dad's bank, and we decided he wouldn't even if he could. But his dad has helped by using his contacts at other banks to help Phil find another position. Recently, he heard of an opportunity in Tulsa and has requested an interview."

"That's good news," Johanna said, "and I'm proud of you and Phil for sticking it out and looking for solutions together." She coughed then continued.

"I want you all to put together another Sunday dinner, this coming Sunday if possible. You'll have to do the work. Or just have the food catered and I'll pay for it. Either way, I want all my family with me while I'm feeling good so we can talk about your future and any possible solutions you need help with. In a few days I'll have my affairs in order, as they say, and we can talk more about plans for your future. Okay? Do you think we can get together on Sunday?"

Stephanie and Erin looked with surprise at their mother. "We can do that, not to worry," Stephanie said. "What else are you talking about? What affairs do you mean? Give us a hint at what you're thinking."

"It's a little complicated and I need some time to think through what we can do. I should be able to talk about it with all the family when we get everyone together."

"Okay," Erin responded. "I'll talk to Will and Christi, and we'll plan a family dinner for Sunday."

The car was quiet the rest of the trip to her Grady County home.

Chapter 36

The family dinner was easy to organize, with everyone eager to do whatever they could to make Johanna comfortable. Will and Christi smoked a brisket, and the others contributed potatoes, a green salad, and two pies for dessert, with a half-gallon of ice cream or a dapple of Cool Whip, if preferred. They laid the food out on the kitchen counter with a stack of dinner plates at one end.

Stephanie's kids grabbed the first plates and started filling their plates. Young Will Jr. was in his highchair with a bib on and banana slices for his first course. Erin followed the youngsters, filling her plate and one for Johanna. As everyone found their place at the long table, Will rolled his mother's wheelchair to her place at the end, then asked everyone to hold hands and bow their heads.

"Father, we thank you for this beautiful day, the food we are about to receive, and for allowing our family to come together. Please sustain us and give us strength through these difficult times, and healing for our mother as she faces a difficult battle ahead. We ask in his name. Amen. Let's eat!"

Johanna spoke. "Thank you all for coming and bringing a wonderful dinner. I don't have the words to express how good it makes me feel to have you all here, all together once again."

The table talk remained positive, avoiding the financial problems in everyone's mind. When the ladies cleared the plates, Stephanie asked her two kids to take Will Jr. into the den and turn on the TV. "The grownups want to talk. We'll call you when dessert is ready."

"I think it would be good for them to hear the McCall family story while I'm still able to tell it," Johanna said. "Why don't you get them some ice cream and we'll get our dessert later?"

Stephanie dipped ice cream for the kids and some adults before settling back to the family table.

Johanna began. "I want all of you to know the history of the McCall family. Fortunately, the day before he died, your father told me more about his grandfather, Thomas McCall, and his story of coming to Oklahoma. It's a bigger story than I originally knew.

"You know your great-grandfather, Thomas, staked this land by participating in the Oklahoma Land Run of 1889; but the story starts in St. Louis, where Thomas grew up during the time of the great westward migration, when pioneer settlers passed through St. Louis to Independence, Missouri and westward on the Oregon Trail, or the California Trail. Most of those pioneers passed up the land called Oklahoma Territory, believing it unfit for farming.

"Later, the government resettled Indian tribes onto reservations in this land nobody wanted. In 1889, the US government announced over a million acres of land previously set aside for Indian reservations would be available for homesteading. In March of that year, Thomas read an article in the *St. Louis Post Dispatch* newspaper reporting the government's plan to open this land on April 22.

"At nineteen years old, Thomas and his friend Francis had been hustling work on the St. Louis docks of the Missouri River, helping westward pioneers transfer to river boats going to Independence on the Oregon or California trail. They wanted to join the westward movement, and when they heard about the opening of lands in Oklahoma Territory, they decided it was the opportunity they'd been waiting for.

"The government offered a quarter section of land, 160 acres, to anyone who would homestead and improve the land over five years. After working it for five years, they would receive clear title to it. To give everyone a fair chance at a land claim, the Land Run of 1889 was organized.

"Thomas and Francis, with their horses weighted down with everything they owned, traveled to the starting line, camping there with thousands of homesteaders waiting for the start. At noon on April 22, a cannon shot at Fort Reno signaled the start of the run. Over fifty thousand farmers, cowboys, bartenders, and cattle rustlers raced to stake their land claim.

"No one knows details of their chaotic run, except that an estimated thousand people were seriously injured or died. Thomas and Francis claimed adjoining quarter section parcels, and the eighty acres this house sits on is part of Thomas's original claim."

"Wow," Erin said. "That's an amazing story. I know the story of the Land Run from Oklahoma history, but I never knew our great-grandfather was part of it."

"Neither did I," Stephanie said. "Go on, Mom. What

happened to Francis? Does his family still own the land he claimed?"

"That, I don't know. We do know that a couple of years after each had built a cabin and made a crop, the KKK raided Francis's farm, burned his home, and killed Francis. Since he hadn't earned title to the land, the government reclaimed the land. The federal land commissioner allowed the local sheriff to claim the land and tried to sign over the title to him. Thomas fought the land grab by the sheriff and used his own land to finance a lawsuit against him.

"Many believed the sheriff was a member of the Klan gang that raided Francis's farm and hung him. Thomas won the lawsuit and gained full title to both claims at the end of the five-year period. Years later, Thomas sold the Francis acreage to pay his debts after several lean farming years. He passed down his quarter section to your grandfather and father. Your father and I lived and worked the farm before selling half of Thomas's original 160 acres to finance the start of McCall's Production Equipment Company back in 1964."

Erin said, "We need to write that story down for future generations."

"We can add to your story," Will interrupted. "Christi, would you like to explain?"

Christi told how her father purchased the eighty acres she believed to be part of Francis's original claim around the same time she met Will, long before they were engaged, and how she and Will had been buying it back from her father.

"My goodness," Johanna said, "I didn't know that. What a wonderful surprise. Lew would be so proud of you. He wasn't a farmer, hated the struggle for meager returns, but he respected the land and believed it a sound investment. As many have said over the years, they're not making any more of it."

"I wish it were that simple and we could say we own it," Christi admitted. "We recently found out my father used the land as part of a letter of credit from his bank that was used to invest in a drilling fund. The fund went bankrupt, and the bank has called his letter of credit and taken title to the property."

"That's disappointing, but maybe we can get it back," Johanna replied. "I've helped Erin and Stephanie financially, and I'll do the same for you and Will. You all know I entered into a drilling lease agreement. Remember, these deep gas wells had a one section spacing requirement, so if a company wanted to drill a deep gas well, they had to receive agreement from all the mineral owners in the 640-acre section, whether drilled on their land or not.

"After the big Tomcat well showed a huge natural gas potential, lease prices skyrocketed. The deal was made with a Texas company called Bluebonnet Oil and Gas for a three-year lease. I consulted with our attorney Sam and an oil and gas attorney in his firm, and later signed a three-year lease with a primary cash payment of 50 percent for access during the first year."

"Outstanding, Mom," Stephanie said. "If I remember our previous discussion, your eighty acres was worth several hundred thousand dollars; and you got half up front?"

Johanna didn't answer her question, but said, "That money will serve to sustain this family for the future. It's due to the conservative investments, commitments, and vision of our McCall ancestors. I feel a responsibility to use it wisely for all in the family, so I've set up a revocable trust as part of my will. That allows me to use the funds as I see fit while I'm alive, with the rest going to you all as beneficiaries when I pass on."

Erin got up from her chair and walked over to her mother, bent down, and gave her a hug. "Our ancestors were tough and resourceful, but you're the one who had the vision to cash in on the land's value for all of us. Thank you."

"She's right," Will said. "You also maintained it was risky for us to take out a business loan in case the deep gas boom turned to a bust, and you were right."

"As I'm sure you expect, Sam Buchanan will be the executor of my estate. He knows my wishes regarding distributing the assets and personal property, all enumerated in my will and trust. In the meantime, I have a plan I want your agreement on.

"Steph, why don't you and the kids move in here with me? I'll need some help in the coming days and I think it would be best if you all move out of that house while your suit to keep title works through the court. We're paying Sam to get the clear title to the house. Later, you can decide whether to move back or sell it for a smaller, more manageable home."

"Thank you, Mom. I think we'd all like that. I know I'd like to be here to help you."

"Will," Johanna continued, "I've paid down the long-term loan on the business, which should help your balance sheet and free up cash to keep the business at breakeven or even turn a small profit in this depressed market. Then, you and Steph and I need to work out a plan to replace me. Paying off the long-term loan should allow you to pay her a salary, and I'll help her get familiar with the business, the suppliers, and the bank."

Johanna turned to Erin. "Sam has also helped Phil and Erin get title to their home. Erin, how is Phil's job search coming? Any new opportunities?"

"Phil hasn't found another bank position. Next Monday, he has an interview with a Tulsa bank. He says it's a long shot but he's staying positive and optimistic."

"All right, I think everybody's financial issues are stable for the moment. I'll meet with each of you in the near future to follow your progress so I can help you if necessary.

"Your grandfather, Bill McCall, was a very hard-working farmer who loved the land he owned and believed that if you took care of it, respected it, didn't take more from it than it yielded, it would sustain you for life. That same lesson relates to the recent boom and bust in our industry. It's a lesson about greed re-learned over and over through the centuries.

"Your Grandfather Bill liked to tell the story of the farmer who wanted more land to increase his wealth, unsatisfied with what he had. One day, a wealthy landowner offered him all the land he could walk in a day, but he must return to the starting point by sunset. So the next morning he started out early, walking quickly to cover the most ground possible. After noon, he picked up his pace to maximize the amount of land he could receive from this once-in-a-lifetime offer to become wealthy. Sound familiar?

"Midafternoon, he remembered the condition that he must return to his starting point by sunset. Unfortunately, his journey had taken him too far away. As he watched the setting sun, he began to run. The closer he got to the starting point, the faster he ran, until he collapsed, totally exhausted, and died at the starting point exactly at sunset. He had gained miles of land, but now all he needed was a small burial plot.

"Greed can drive you to sacrifice everything you cherish for things you don't need. Greed makes you pay a high price for things without caring about your health or the wellbeing of your family. This story is a human one, not exclusive to you or Americans. All philosophers and religions, through the centuries, have warned against the transient nature of goods and the impermanence of things.

"We are only stewards of the land and its resources. If we care for them, they can sustain us long into the future. Let's be content with what we have and share it where there is need."

Chapter 37

Stephanie began working at the offices of McCall's. As the former business manager of C&S Trucking and Sooner Oil and Gas, she had experience in bookkeeping and as a purchasing agent. Learning about the employees, their pay, and the personnel records system was her only challenge. She often took records and questions to Johanna for her advice and answers on personnel matters.

After only two or three weeks, Stephanie needed little help, but Johanna was finding it difficult to break away from the business she helped build for the last fifteen years. On the days she had enough energy, she would drop in to see how Stephanie and the business were doing.

Though thankful to have the job and receive a salary, Stephanie remained bitter about her situation. Charley left her with a mortgage and expenses that her bookkeeping salary barely covered, leaving little extra for herself and the children.

Johanna invested most of the lease money in bank CDs, holding back a few thousand to help her family. It was late morning the following Sunday when Stephanie and Erin arrived at her house to check on her. They found her in the den, lying on the couch in her housecoat and slippers.

"Mom! Are you okay?" Erin asked.

"Yes, I'm fine, just a little tired."

"Did you have breakfast this morning?"

"Yes and no. I got up and went in to fix some bacon and eggs when I felt a little faint and had to lay down."

"Do you feel like getting up and sitting in the kitchen chair?" Stephanie asked. "Erin and I can fix something to eat while we talk. We're concerned about just this sort of thing."

"It's a little early for lunch," Erin observed, "but I'll see if we can heat up some soup and make a sandwich. You need protein to get your energy back." She headed to the kitchen with tears in her eyes.

"I need to get up," Johanna said, straining to sit up and slide her feet to the floor. "I'm hungry, but just don't have the energy to cook."

"You can rest longer if you need to. I'm sorry we didn't get here sooner to help you."

"Thank you. But I want to get up now."

Stephanie helped her to her feet. "Are you okay? Stand there a second, steady yourself. Take my arm and we'll walk into the kitchen. Erin and I have talked about the possibility you'll need some daily help. Your experience today means it's time for that. I think you'd be safer and more comfortable if you had a few hours of day care on weekdays when we can't be here to help you with your normal routine. We'll take turns coming in on the weekend."

With Stephanie's help Johanna shuffled into the kitchen and eased into a chair at the table. "Honey, I'm fine most of the time, but I do get concerned when I feel weak. I'm okay with whatever works best for you two."

"Mom, you offered for us to move over here, but it's going to be difficult with the kids in school. Sam Buchanan says getting the deed for the house in my name requires some paperwork that will be completed soon. So there's no immediate pressure to move out. My biggest concern is that you get the help and care you need, care and attention Erin and I are not trained to provide."

Erin added, "Phil is going to be traveling to interviews, job hunting, which would free me up to move in here with you. But Stephanie's right. You need and deserve professional care."

Stephanie then offered their next plan. "We think you should request hospice services. Hospice is a new in-home nursing service for patients like you that wish to stay home. They come in several times a week to administer pain medicines and nursing care. Things Erin and I aren't qualified to do. They'll even prepare a meal or two. Many of their patients are on Medicare insurance, which pays for their services, and I'm told we can pay for the same services if they accept you into the program."

Johanna agreed, adding that she had enough money to afford the service. There was no need for her daughters to squeeze the hospice fees out of their limited incomes.

Within a week, a hospice nurse was engaged to visit Johanna three times a week, with Stephanie and Erin alternating daily checks the other two days and weekends. Johanna had pain medicine with instructions on how to increase the dosage if needed.

Phil drove to Tulsa that first hospice week and Erin got a call from him Friday afternoon. "I just finished an interview with First National Bank of Tulsa and wanted you to know I'm headed home," he reported to her. "How's everything there?"

"We're fine, no new family news. The hospice care nurse we hired for Mom is working out well. How did your bank interview go?"

"It went well. They just don't have loan officer positions open. Their loan business is down, like all banks in Oklahoma, so they're not hiring any loan officers. I've also decided it's a waste of time to try for an appointment at Utica Square National Bank. They're in trouble on several oil and gas deals, much the same as Oak Tree. I'm at a Phillips station to get gas, then I'll be on the turnpike headed home. Thank goodness we still have gas money. See you in a couple of hours."

Meanwhile, Will and Christi faced foreclosure on the eighty acres of land purchased by Christi's father and financed through his bank. Christi's name was on the deed, but the property was an asset in a standby letter of credit issued in her father's name and called by a bankrupt drilling fund. As part of Johanna's commitment to help her children during this financial crisis, she asked Sam Buchanan to intervene on Christi's behalf. Christi told him she never agreed to the letter of credit, yet she was the one making the payments on the mortgage loan.

"I think we can negotiate a settlement in your favor, since the bank really doesn't want to claim the land," Sam said. "They're not in the real estate business and don't want to try to sell the property in this poor economic environment. I'm betting they'll accept a discounted balance on the mortgage, which could easily be refinanced since two-thirds of the principal has been paid."

Chapter 38

During painful emotional trauma, time slows down. Hours and days creep by in agony. During Johanna's last days, family members gathered around their mother's bed to comfort her as much as they could. Her pain was under control, and the meds allowed brief moments of consciousness, during which her children and grandchildren could be with her to express their love for a mother and grandmother who raised them and now was helping them avoid financial ruin.

Johanna Mueller McCall died peacefully in her sleep. Funeral arrangements included her cremated ashes to be interred in the Lutheran church columbarium next to Lew's. Friends and family attended the memorial service and reception at Will and Christi's home, with the noticeable absence of Charley and JD Arnold.

At the family dinner that evening, they toasted Johanna and her life several times with stories of happier times, each remembering funny moments and life lessons she offered. Each of her children followed her desire to celebrate her life. No tears, no sadness, no regrets.

Stephanie and Christi were placing the last dishes of food on the table when Erin called everyone to gather around to hold hands and give thanks.

"Before we give thanks, I want to share this poem as we celebrate Mom's life with us. The author is a Canadian, Christy Ann Martine, who has published several beautiful, soulful writings. I think it says what was in Mom's heart."

Don't cry for me, I am not gone,
My soul is at rest, my heart lives on.
Light a candle for me to see
And hold on to my memory.
But save your tears, for I am still here
By your side through the years.

"That was beautiful, Erin," Will said. "Thank you, and now let us give thanks."

An enthusiastic "Let's eat" followed his words of thanks to the Lord.

It got quiet around the family table as everyone consumed the smoked brisket, baked potatoes, Caesar salad, and King Hawaiian rolls.

When most plates were empty, Stephanie announced, "I'm happy to report my house is now in my name, and although I still have a mortgage to pay off, we're glad the house is ours and we can stay there or sell it, which I'm planning to do. We'll find a home we can afford, easier and cheaper to maintain, and add some personal touches to make it our own."

"That's wonderful, Steph," Erin replied. "Phil and I have good news, too. We're moving to Tulsa."

"What!" Stephanie exclaimed. "Where did that come from? You guys have been holding out on us."

"You tell 'em, Phil," Erin answered.

"It's the result of networking, and a little luck," Phil

explained. "When I returned from an interview at the First National Bank in Tulsa several weeks ago, I told Christi's dad about the interview. He told me there were unconfirmed reports that Liberty Bank was talking to First National Tulsa about a merger. Later, I was able to get an appointment with a senior VP. After introductions, he went right into his knowledge of my work as a loan officer at Oak Tree.

"I was immediately discouraged as he explained why they have no need for another loan officer when they were cutting costs and trying to reduce their loan portfolio. Then, I pointed to my résumé detailing my experience and performance working with Continental Illinois Trust in Chicago and how I could be helpful in disposing of at-risk loans if they decide to merge with the Tulsa bank.

"He became more interested, less defensive. We met a couple of days later, discussed the responsibilities of the position and compensation, and he offered me the job. More details are to be worked out. I'll do some traveling, and I'm excited, confident I've got the experience and skill set they need."

"Phil, that's great news," Will replied. "Congratulations to both of you. What a great opportunity, and I know you'll do well."

Applause and well-wishes followed from everyone.

"Also," Will said, "I want to give you an update on the status of Mom's will. Sam Buchanan has submitted it to the probate judge for approval and expects it to be released to all beneficiaries this coming week. As we did with Dad's, Sam has asked us to come together to review the terms and its dispensation. You can expect a cover letter with the copy and a couple of suggested dates for that meeting. Please reply to him when you can meet and ask any questions.

"One last thing. Christi has good news."

"Will and I are pregnant again. We're expecting in April." More applause and congratulations followed.

Chapter 39

Sam sent Stephanie, Will, and Erin each a written invitation along with a copy of the will in a sealed envelope and a note saying, "To be opened during the reading of Johanna Mueller McCall's will."

Johanna's children and their spouses arrived at Sam's offices a few minutes before the agreed time and, one by one, were escorted to the familiar executive conference room.

Will and Christie arrived first and took executive chairs near the head of the familiar long, walnut conference table. Christi turned to give him an update on what her title search of their acreage uncovered a couple of weeks ago.

"You remember I told you I learned the mineral rights on our property in Grady County were owned by your mother. An additional title search of past county records show the minerals were passed down several generations from your great-grandfather, Thomas, to your grandfather, then your father and mother. When we learned at the picnic that she leased her minerals to the Texas operator, she never said how much they paid her. Stephanie calculated it could be close to a quarter of a million, based on the eighty acres. If the lease also included the minerals on our eighty acres, she would have gotten twice as much."

"Wow, you're right. Her estate could be much larger than we expect. On the other hand, Mom has helped all of us with legal fees, mortgage payments, loans, and whatnot. That probably took much of the money."

Stephanie arrived dressed casually in a blouse, slacks, and white tennis shoes. She greeted them cordially and took a leather chair across from them. She'd pushed back from the table with arms folded, looking at a sealed envelope with a frown.

Erin and Phil followed, dressed almost formally, Phil in a sport coat and Erin in a lovely print dress. They took seats next to Stephanie and greeted everyone, asking Christi how she was feeling.

Sam came in moments later, closed the door, and laid down a thick file and notepad at the head of the table.

He went around to greet each one and thank them for coming. "I'm glad to see you all have your sealed copy of your mother's will with instruction not to open it. This procedure was Johanna's request, and you'll understand her reasons as we proceed."

"Sam, before you start, I have a question," Will said, gesturing with open hands. "Isn't this a living trust, wherein Mom's assets transfer at time of death to us, the beneficiaries? And if so, why the secrecy? Isn't it all done as written by her?"

"I agree," Stephanie said. "And we don't have any choice in the matter, right?"

"You are correct. Johanna McCall's will is part of a living trust which transfers her estate assets upon her death to her beneficiaries. There are also claims, debts, and local taxes that will be paid from the estate. I have made a detailed accounting of all those and will take care of those claims as her designated executor.

"Stephanie, I know you have concerns about how your mother's shares in the company are going to be handled. You may even have thoughts about challenging the will, but I think all of you will be happy after covering the complete terms and her wishes.

"As the executer of her will, I will administer the trust as she wished. She wanted you all to be together when her will was read. That's the reason I asked you to bring your copy unopened. Any other questions? If not, I'll proceed by reading a summary before you open your copies."

"Let's begin with the dispensation of her home and property. Johanna bequeaths the home and land in Grady County to her oldest daughter, Stephanie McCall Arnold. Her car will be sold, and funds added to the liquid value of the estate. Her personal property goes to individual beneficiaries, as listed. Shares of stock in the company go to William McCall, and his loan balance forgiven for shares he was buying from his sisters. He will now be the sole owner of McCall's Production Equipment Company. To Paul Smith, the company's longtime shop supervisor, she leaves twenty-five thousand dollars. To Erin McCall Pederson, she gives the equity value of their home as part of recovering the deed and mortgage at First City Bank."

Erin squeezed Phil's hand, and they smiled at each other. Stephanie had straightened up in her chair with her hand to her mouth, partially covering her look of surprise. Will and Christi were also smiling.

Sam continued, "To her grandchildren, she

bequeaths an education trust fund in the amount of $30,000 to be established for each grandchild, including any unborn or adopted."

Sam was about to continue when Stephanie interrupted. "Hold on, Sam. Where is all this money coming from? There are three grandchildren already, Christie's pregnant with another, and we just learned Erin and Phil are adopting a little girl. That's five education trust funds. We knew of the drilling lease she sold, expecting she got something over two hundred thousand, but figure much of that she spent paying off a company loan and helping us with our financial problems. Unless she had some huge savings account unknown to us, the addition of the education trusts would seem to exceed what we thought her estate is worth."

"Your mother expected one of you might raise that question before I finished." Sam said. "If you all will open the envelope to a letter behind her instructions to me. There is a letter to all of you that will answer Stephanie's question and explain the value of her estate."

Dearest Stephanie, Will, and Erin,

The value of my estate is the rest of the McCall family story.

You know the history of your ancestor, Thomas McCall, fighting for his land and that of his best friend, Francis. Through the years, he sold much of the land to cover debts following lean years. Lew inherited Thomas's original quarter section from his father, and later we sold half of it, eighty acres, to start the family business.

What I didn't know until just before your father's

death was that rights to the underground minerals on Thomas's quarter section and Francis's quarter section were passed down to your father and then to me.

In Oklahoma, you can hold the in-ground minerals in a separate deed while selling the surface land separately. When I sold the lease rights to the Texas operator, the contract was for $4200 per acre for all the minerals for a term of three years, and I received half in cash for the first year's rights. That first-year option expired earlier this year.

The amount remaining from that cash payment of $672,000, after taxes, debts and other specific grants are paid, and my grandchildren's education funds set aside, will be distributed accordingly: Erin McCall Pederson will receive one-half. Stephanie McCall Arnold and William Lewis McCall will split the other half equally.

I've had a good life, a wonderful husband, and a beautiful family. Now, I can face my maker knowing I've helped all of you into the future.

Love, Mom

"Oh, my goodness," Erin exclaimed.

Stephanie was leaning on the conference table with tears filling her wide-open eyes and hands covering her mouth.

"Wow, Sam," Will said. "We didn't know the family owned that many acres of minerals, or their value. Can you tell us how much we will share after all loans and debts are settled and the grandchildren's trusts established?"

"The total remaining will be approximately three hundred thousand," Sam said. "I think you also understand why the split favors Erin. Stephanie receives your mother's home and land, and you get total ownership of McCall's Process Equipment Company."

"How about taxes? Will we owe taxes on that money?"

"No," Sam said. "Her home and property, plus the lease money, are in the living trust. Other personal property and stock in McCall's Production and Equipment Company outside the trust did not exceed the estate tax threshold, so there is no estate tax due. She paid the tax on the lease income and the balance was placed in the living trust along with her house, land, and a few remaining investments she had made from the life insurance on your father."

"She had money left from his life insurance?" Stephanie questioned. "I thought Dad's life insurance was only about two hundred thousand dollars, and we know she spent money finishing the house after his death."

"Yes," Sam replied, "but it paid twice that much under a double-indemnity clause for accidental death. And she invested the money wisely, which offset the large tax bill on the lease income."

Stephanie, wiping tears from her cheek, said, "I'm such a jerk. Please forgive me for the way I behaved earlier. I don't know what I was expecting, but it wasn't this. Once again, Mom was right, and the wisest of us all."

Chapter 40

Friday of the following week, Stephanie was in her office of McCall's Production Equipment and got a call from George Martin.

"Good morning, George. Are we late paying an invoice again? I thought we were up to date with Vinson."

"No, you're fine, and we're happy McCall's is surviving this downturn in the industry. We lost several small customers to bankruptcy, and we deal in only cash with other accounts in financial trouble. No, I'm calling to see if you take a lunch break. My day is open, and I wondered if you'd like to join me for lunch."

"Wow, how nice. Yes, I would enjoy getting together for lunch. What time?"

"I'll come by about eleven thirty. Will that work for you?"

"Yes, perfectly. I'll see you then." She hung up. *How nice. I've never thought of George as someone I'd date, but I'm flattered and excited. Ready to move on with my life.*

Phil's new job allowed him and Erin to stay in Oklahoma City for the foreseeable future. Erin stayed busy decorating their small bedroom in shades of pink with a custom wall painting of Snow White. The adoption of their baby girl was almost final. They spent a portion of their inheritance upgrading their home, now legally theirs with a mortgage that fit their budget.

Will knew he needed to find new products to manufacture if his business was to survive the depressed oil and gas market. Ironically, he found a new product opportunity making natural gas fuel tanks for commercial vehicles. Compressed natural gas was getting considerable interest as an alternative fuel, particularly for daily, short run fleet vehicles like UPS trucks that are refueled overnight. The fuel tank need to be a thick-walled steel cylinder to hold the gas under pressure, and McCall's had the facilities to make them. Someday, personal cars might switch to natural gas, a clean burning fuel for internal combustion engines.

This potential market had him excited and working on the designs for the fuel cylinders when Paul Smith came into his office one day.

"Will, I'd like to retire at the end of the year. I'm giving notice now so you and I can find a suitable replacement. I don't think we have an excellent candidate in our current shop group, so we'll probably need to search outside for a shop supervisor."

"Paul, I have to say I'm disappointed, but I wish you all the best and appreciate the heads-up on leaving. You're still young and in good health. What are your plans?"

"To see the USA in my Chevrolet," he said with a big smile, mocking a frequent TV ad. "I'm buying a motor home and planning a tour of the U. S. of A. for at least six months. Longer, if all goes well. Regarding my replacement, I've made some inquiries among other shops to find qualified candidates and made a list for you to consider. Let me know how you want to do this and how I can help."

"Thanks, Paul. That's a tremendous help, and I definitely want your input on all prospective people we interview. I'll want you to talk with each, show them our shop, and give me your opinion on their experience and ability to do your job."

Over the next two weeks, Will interviewed several candidates for the shop supervisor position, and another interviewee arrived this morning.

Betty called Will and said, "Jack Ruggles is here for an interview. Are you ready for him?" She received a positive response and escorted him to Will's office.

"Good morning, Jack," Will said and offered his hand. "Would you like some coffee?"

Betty answered for him. "He said he drinks his black. Can I get you a refill, Will?"

"Yes, thank you, Betty." He handed her his favorite mug, *Oil Field Trash*.

"I've read your résumé, Jack, and see you worked for National Tank Company in Tulsa. What brings you to us?"

"We want to get back to my family farm, southeast of here in Seminole County. My grandfather homesteaded the farm and my parents inherited it from him. They've both passed on and it's been rented the past few years. They shut in the producing oil well on the property and capped it in 1969. Our plan is to move back there and fix up the old farmhouse. I plan on commuting to work in this area."

"Now I know why the name Ruggles rang a bell with me," Will said. "Was your father Joe Dan Ruggles?"

"Why, yes. Did you know him?"

"Not really. I met him at the well site that Phillips shut down on your property in the summer of 1969, right after my father passed away. In fact, my visit to the site that day marked the start of my work in this company my father started two decades ago. If you have time, I'll share the story while I give you a tour of our shop."

"Interesting," the young Mr. Ruggles said. "Yes, I'd like to know more."

—The End

Epilogue

Following the collapse of Penn Square Bank in 1982, sixty-nine banks in Oklahoma fell like dominoes over the next five years. Several Penn Square officers were indicted for fraud, but most avoided jail time. The banking failure extended to the First National Bank of Midland Texas, United American Bank of Knoxville, Seattle First National, and Continental Illinois Trust of Chicago—which was one of the largest banks in the United States at that time and the largest bank in history to fail, taken over by the FDIC.

C. W. "Cliff Culpepper moved to California and continued to battle debts that totaled over $30 million. Many years later he return to Oklahoma City, where he died in 2004. Though never a commercial success, the Tomcat #1 remains one of the biggest natural gas strikes in history.

Vinson Supply Company, a major supplier of down hole casing to Ports of Call and many others, during the drilling boom was one of United States Steel's largest customers by tonnage in 1981, surpassed only by General Motors. After the bust, Vinson was left with millions in casing inventory but unlike most suppliers to the boom, they survived because they had no debt.

About the Author

Monty McGinnis is a retired sales engineer who spent much of his forty-year career in Oklahoma selling control valves and measurement instruments to oil and gas production companies such as Phillips Petroleum, Conoco, and Kerr-McGee.

Gas Money is based on actual historical events of the '70s and early '80s.

REFERENCES

Berry, John M. "With Tom Cat #1, All's Well for Washington Gas Light Co." *Washington Post*, April 21, 1981.

Boyd, Dean T. "Oklahoma Oil: Past, Present, and Future." *Sipes Quarterly*, February 2009. Rev. from *Shale Shaker*, May/June 2008.

Oklahoma Historical Society. n.d. "Removal of Tribes to Oklahoma." Accessed January 17, 2022. https://www.okhistory.org/research/airemoval.

Singer, Mark. *Funny Money*. 2004 ed. New York: Mariner Books, Houghton Mifflin Company, 1985.

Spanbock, Ben. n.d. "The Oklahoma Land Run Then and Now." Accessed January 17, 2022. http://www.benspanbock.net/oklahoma-land-run.html.

U.S. Energy Information Administration. n.d. "U.S. Natural Gas Wellhead Price 1975-2010." Accessed January 17, 2022. https://www.eia.gov/dnav/ng/hist/n9190us3m.htm.

Wells, B.A. and K.L. Wells. "Anadarko Basin in Depth." American Oil and Gas Historical Society (website). Last Updated: April 11, 2021. https://aoghs.org/technology/anadarko-basin-depth.

Zeig, Phillip L. *Belly Up: The Collapse of Penn Square Bank*. New York: Fawcett Columbine, Ballentine Books, 1985.

Made in the USA
Monee, IL
15 May 2022

96340285R00163